I0691399

The Butler &
the Barbarians

First Edition

Published by The Nazca Plains Corporation
Las Vegas, Nevada
2010

ISBN: 978-1-935509-36-3

Published by

The Nazca Plains Corporation ®
4640 Paradise Rd, Suite 141
Las Vegas NV 89109-8000

© 2010 by The Nazca Plains Corporation. All rights reserved.
No part of this work may be reproduced or utilized in any form or
by any means, electronic or mechanical, including photocopying,
microfilm, and recording, or by any information storage and retrieval
system, without permission in writing from the publisher. Printed in
the United States of America.

PUBLISHER'S NOTE
The Butler & the Barbarians is a work of fiction created wholly
by *Bob Archman's* imagination. All characters are fictional and any
resemblance to any persons living or deceased is purely by accident.
No portion of this book reflects any real person or events.

Cover Male Photo, MAXFX
Art Director, Blake Stephens

DEDICATION

To the men who lose everything and then find themselves.

The Butler & the Barbarians

First Edition

Bob Archman

CONTENTS

CHAPTER ONE

Escape

The world was coming to an end and Hadrian decided to go to the baths. The small band of men sent to repel the Saxons had been defeated and refugees from Londinium and other cities to the south and east had spread the word the barbarians were on the way. Panic griped the ancient city of Verulamium, and hundreds fled to the north and west, hoping the wilderness of Wales and of the Pict lands would afford some protection.

The baths were almost empty except for a few men, most of whom were old friends. The water still ran and the men who stoked the furnace had not fled yet. The warm water seemed to invite Hadrian to relax. He stripped in the changing room and walked naked into the warm caldarium, and got in the water next to Julian, the smith. Julian was sitting in a cluster of four bearded men, three blond, one dark haired.

Julian was his best friend. They weren't lovers anymore, but they still knew how to have a good time, and enjoyed each other's company as friends and playmates. "We who are about to die salute you!" exclaimed Hadrian. Julian was not impressed.

"You haven't fled yet?" Julian asked.

"No the master and his family have left for the Pict Land where they have relatives. They took the servants they liked and left me to deal with the Saxons," answered Hadrian.

"I bet the Saxons would find you attractive. They say Saxons like anything they can fuck," bantered Julian.

Hadrian replied, "They may, but I can't figure out how to get their cocks up my ass before they chop off my head." There was a titter of laughter at the end of the pool.

"Maybe we could label you as a guy who likes cock?" suggested Julian.

"I am afraid they can't read," answered Hadrian, "You know I don't care who is fucking me as long as his cock is big. I have sampled barbarian cock in my time, but I'm afraid I had better get on my way to a safer locale."

"I've been thinking the same thing myself, but I don't know where to go. The Boys don't seem to have any thoughts themselves." Julian retained his bantering tone, but there was a tinge of desperation in his voice. The Boys were men who worked with Julian, the men who sat next to him in the pool. He referred to them as his harem, but not in their presence. Hadrian knew them only as Wolf, Fox, Badger and Otter, all Britons, very different from the Middle Eastern Julian or the Italian Hadrian. Not one of the men was native to this part of Britannia and none had family nearby.

Hadrian lay back in the warm water and fondled Julian to his right and Otter to his left. Julian was used to the touch, but Otter responded well, and began to play with Hadrian' cock and with Wolf, who was on the other side. Every one's cock responded immediately to the stimulation, but the conversation above the water continued.

"Do you think there is any chance the Saxons would let us live?" asked Wolf.

"They seem to like young children who they can adopt and young women they can fuck, but a tall, mustached, hairy British man has no chance. The only question will be whether they kill you slow or fast," volunteered Otter. Otter relocated in the pool, dipped under the water for a second, and emerged for a breath of air. At the same time, he worked a finger into Wolf and Hadrian's ass. Soon they were having a hard time carrying on the conversation without moaning in pleasure.

"We need to go somewhere, I am not going to stay here and get slaughtered." Everyone agreed with Fox, who, since no one was fondling or finger fucking him, seemed to have a clearer view of the situation.

"I know a place!" Hadrian stood up so fast he trapped Otter's finger in his ass. "It's a villa, on the sea!" He was fully erect, and while Julian had seen him many times, the Boys were interested. Otter pushed his finger in deeper and made contact with Hadrian's prostate. This left the older man speechless for a moment. At the other end of the pool, the Presbyter Maximus and the Magistrate Optimus took notice of the sexual drama at the other end. They were engaged in their own sexual exploration. When they rose from the pool, both were half-erect. They joined the small group at the other end.

Hadrian admired big men, and the cocks he saw walking toward him were everything he liked in a cock. He sat down and greeted the two men. They all knew each other by sight, and so they were familiar, but had been unaware they shared common sexual interests. "Join us friends!" exclaimed Julian. "We are plotting our escape from this fair city." He beckoned to the men, inviting them to sit between him and Hadrian. They took the offer, sat and immediately grabbed their neighbor's cocks.

"What place?" asked Maximus.

Hadrian lost his thought as the firm hand of the Presbyter took hold of his cock and Otter massaged his prostate. "The Villa! Tell us about the villa!" Julian cried trying to get him to resume his earlier thought.

"On the sea, about three days from here, very secluded, almost hidden." Hadrian tried to sound calm as his cock and ass responded to the stimulation.

"Who lives there?" asked Maximus.

"It's been abandoned about two, or three years I think, ever since the southern slave insurrection. I worked there about twenty years ago. I was a wonderful villa, filled with secret compartments, chambers and grottoes. Even if it is destroyed, I know the countryside well. It's filled with caves. There will be someplace to hide," answered Hadrian.

All of the men were alone, far from their families, tribes or clans. They had few options for escape. Most of the Britons were notoriously clannish, and were unlikely to give shelter to strangers. Distant cousins and uncles fleeing from the barbarian advance over whelmed most of the country families to the north and west. They had no room for others.

Common sexual interests also linked the men gathered in the warm pool. Perhaps the civilized world was coming to an end and Rome was falling, but as the barbarians advanced on this minor provincial city in Britannia, at least the men could all maintain an erection.

There were screams outside the bath. An attendant ran in and said he saw smoke on the horizon. "I guess it is time to go!" Julian stood; his erection had not survived the imminent threat of death.

"To the Villa?" asked Wolf. They all ran to the dressing room, quickly dressed and left the bath. Outside all was disorder, panic everywhere. There was the smell of smoke. The time for discussion was over and the eight men ran to the northern gate to the city and then into the countryside.

They ran north and then began a slow turn left and then headed to the southern coast of Britain. At first there had been hundreds of panicking refugees, but soon the numbers diminished. All of the bathers were strong men, and they continued to push ahead as the weaker fell behind. They also fled with little more than the clothes on their backs, so they weren't burdened with possessions, wives or children.

The land had once been fertile and prosperous, but the slow decline of the last decades had taken its toll. Abandoned farms, villas and fields covered the area. Second growth vegetation choked the fields and made travel slow. It also must have slowed the Saxons, who were nowhere evident. Otter, Fox and Wolf were good hunters, and the Presbyter had a knack for finding edible food.

After three days, they were well away from the city, and were able to relax a little. It was early summer; the weather was good. Oddly, the sense that everything they had known for their entire lives was gone, and they were stranded, alone and isolated, seemed liberating.

The nearness of death and the physical exertion of the flight drove the thoughts of sexual adventure from Hadrian's mind for the first time in years. Fears and anxieties consumed him. He was the default leader, since he had both a plan and a destination. He really didn't know if the villa still existed. Its patrician residents might be still live there, or it might be the stronghold of a Saxon chieftain. Furthermore, the depopulation of the countryside and the creeping underbrush made it difficult to find old familiar landmarks.

He figured if he went south they eventually would encounter the sea, and the villas would necessarily be to the east or west. He felt great relief when they encountered a burned villa he recognized as being about a half days travel from the Villa by the sea. It was burned and abandoned, human remains, scattered about by dogs made it clear the original residents had either all been killed or fled too far to return. There was no sign of any more recent residents, Roman, British or barbarian.

Hadrian relaxed knowing at least he was in the right district. He had spent a week in the house serving his master who was a houseguest. He remembered the fields, filled with vegetables, fruits and vines, and the location of the wine cellar. He sent most of the group of men off to scavenge, something must have remained, a fruit tree or berry patch. He and Optimus went looking for the wine. "It only gets better with age," he thought.

The cellar was hidden deep inside the house with a concealed entrance, known only by the owner, his wife and the chief butler. The owner was obsessed with the fear the slaves would rob him, so had taken exceptional precautions. Hadrian had discovered it when the chief butler conceived a great passion for him, (Hadrian looked younger than his age at the time, and did a superb imitation of an innocent virgin boy just discovering his sexual interests and looking for a teacher.)

The butler needed some uninterrupted training time, and the cellar was the best place, far away from his wife or lovers. The entrance was under a mosaic of Mars and Venus in the dining room. Hadrian looked for the room, but could not find it at first. The heavy tile roof had collapsed in the fire that destroyed the villa, and every room seemed to look alike. Hadrian tried to retrace his steps of twenty years earlier. A pile of glass tiles on the floor indicated the site of the ruined mosaic, and the two men cleared away the burned beams of the ceiling to gain access to the cellar entrance.

Hadrian pushed the hidden door; it resisted then creaked open. The appalling stench of rotted and decayed flesh surged into the air. Hadrian closed the door. He knew the fate of the Villa's residents. Optimus wanted to investigate further, a scientific curiosity took charge of his common sense. Hadrian would not stay in the room, and as Optimus did not want to be alone in the room possibly inhabited by the spirits of the dead, they both left.

The two men had never been alone together, and had only known each other by sight in the baths. As often happened in the baths, they had seen each other naked, and on the last day, erect, but had never been introduced. "Do you know these men?" asked Optimus of their traveling companions.

"Julian and I are old friends," answered Hadrian, "He has described the boys, but I had never met them. How long have you and the Presbyter been friends?"

"Fox seems particularly attractive to me," Optimus replied, "but I don't know if he is Julian's lover."

"I'm sure he is, but Julian is a big man with many passions, and imaginative too. I can't believe they aren't all his lovers, or there isn't any combination of cock, asshole and mouth he hasn't tried. When we were lovers, he used to search out big cocks to fuck me, so he could watch me squirm. He loved groups, no holes bared, and I will say, he could always take anything or anyone in the room," explained Hadrian. "What about the Presbyter? You haven't answered my question."

"I met him eight or so years ago. At the baths, we enjoyed each other's company. Seeing a clergyman naked was exciting. He was the first and only man to fuck me; I couldn't believe the feelings. I had believed a man of my rank should always be the top, it was disgraceful to take a cock in the ass. At one time, I thought I was doing my bit for God as Maximus screwed me. Now I know I am doing it for me." Hadrian reached down and rubbed the doctor's crotch, and discovered he had an erection. He was not at all surprised. "But lately, I seem to be obsessed with dreams of common men, and common cocks," concluded Optimus. He did not object to his companion rubbing his member.

"If we live through this, let me promise you, you will have had every man in the group in your ass sometime in the near future," Hadrian spoke confidently. They heard the rustling of leaves and the scavenging party returned.

"Fruits and nuts!" exclaimed Wolf. "Enough for a week!" Hadrian confessed his failure at finding the wine cellar, but the group settled down to wolfing the food.

Good food brought back old feelings of lust to Hadrian. He had been surprised as the size of the magistrate's equipment, as he had been three days earlier at the bath by the erect Presbyter. Even in his excited state as Otter squeezed the juice out of his prostate Hadrian had been impressed. He had a lot of experience with common men, and some with men of rank, mostly officers in the Legions, but none with scholars and priests. If they lived, there were many opportunities to explore.

The men ate and then went to sleep, with two keeping watch as the others slept. They had tried having one man watching, but discovered it was too easy to fall into sleep. Two could keep each other awake. Maximus and Badger were the first watch.

Maximus was tall and impressive, with dark thinning hair. The robes he wore made him look thin but that was because his shoulders were wider than his waist, and the clothes tended to hang on him. Badger was short, reddish blond and bearded. Quite muscular, and with his old clothes in tatters after the three days of running through briar's and brambles, much of his body was visible. He was a Briton, but from the East Coast. He had never spoken to a man of the Presbyter's rank before.

After a long period of silence, the bigger man's head nodded forward, and then jerked up again. This happened several times then he whispered, "Badger."

"Yes Sir?"

"Are you awake?"

"Yes sir, no problem."

"How do you do it? How do you stay awake? I am exhausted," Maximus added.

Badger came closer. He whispered, "Do you want the secret?"

"I need something, are you accustomed to keeping watch?" Maximus asked.

Badger came even closer, rubbing against the bigger man's leg. "No, but you might not approve of my method of keeping alert; it was taught to me by a Pictish boy I knew."

"Why wouldn't I approve? How can staying awake on watch be a matter of approval?" Maximus was annoyed, but noticed the little man was humping his leg with a full sized erection.

"Keep yourself excited; keep your cock up and dripping. But don't shoot. Just keep on the edge."

The Presbyter was going to say something sharp, when he realized the erect cock rubbing his leg had woken him up, and is own cock was inflating. "Shit, you're right. It does wake you up."

"It sure does, and it can keep you awake as long as you just don't shoot. Keep it all in the balls." Badger smiled. "Pop when you go off watch and you will sleep like a baby." He felt and rubbed the presbyter's cock. The sexual tension had eliminated all of the drowsiness.

"How long can you go? I have never gone long before going over the edge."

"Julian, the boys and I can go for a whole evening or all night without losing interest. We stay awake and at least half erect," answered Badger. He loosened his belt and let the tatters of his clothes fall open, Maximus reached down and felt the hard cock and the big cock head oozing pre-cum. It was bigger than he had expected in the small man. In the moonlight, Badger's well-muscled body was visible below the thick coat of blond hair covering it. Badger reached to his own cock, ran his finger around the head and collected pre-cum, then raised it to his mouth and tasted it. "If you get tired, take a lick of your juice and you will wake again," he volunteered.

"I can't believe that!" the priest seemed shocked. Badger reached down again, collected a second batch of the slippery ooze, and raised it to Maximus' mouth. He forced the finger into the unwilling mouth.

Maximus was appalled, and then he found himself sucking the finger as if it were his mother breast. He felt wild with excitement. "My god," he explained, "unbelievable!" The diminutive Badger looked up and smiled. Maximus felt warm and excited; he felt driven. "Can I have more?" he asked. Badger smiled again. Maximus suddenly realized another drip on a finger was not enough, he wanted more; he needed more. He was on his knees, and engulfed the small man's cock in one movement. His tongue searched out the ooze wherever it was, on the head, in the foreskin, trying to get deep in the piss slit.

Badger was amused at first, but amusement soon changed to intense excitement. He started to pump. Maximus held onto Badger's balls to steady himself, and Badger let loose days of over ripe British cum. Maximus had his tongue in the piss slit and felt seed trying to escape from the balls and held it back briefly. It felt as if something was trying to tickle his tongue inside the slit. Badger was twitching as his semen was trapped between the balls and the head. Max relaxed the pressure and this mouth was flooded with warm salty man juice. Badger was almost crying with passion and release. Maximus had never felt anything like this in his years of playing with Optimus.

Here Max was sucking the life juice from a common blacksmith's apprentice. The Presbyter's lips had never touched another man's cock. "I'm sorry," said Badger, "I told you not to shoot and I just did."

The Priest almost said, "I forgive you my son," but suddenly wasn't sure forgiveness was needed. They were alone, fleeing from the barbarian hoards, not knowing it anything survived of hundreds of years of Roman civilization. Was giving pleasure to another man a sin? They were not children, being exploited and used. He could not imagine Badger could have felt more pleasure, and he certainly felt more pure enjoyment than he had ever felt before.

He continued his rather confused musings as they resumed their watch. The moon had risen high and was beginning to set. He looked over to Badger and saw his head slump, then jerk up alert. Maximus quietly moved nearer, reached into his robe and ran his finger over his pre-cum coating his cock head. He took the finger and touched Badger's mouth, and stuck it in. Badger sucked it greedily. Their watch was up, but they would be many more watches in the future.

Julian and Wolf were on the next watch. They were playmates rather than lovers. Indeed all of the Boys were playmates. The two men were physical opposites. Wolf was tall, lean and lank, with black hair streaked with white. His long hair merged with his beard and then mingled with his hairy chest and shoulders. Julian was short, stocky and muscular as befit a blacksmith who spent every working hour exercising his upper body with the heavy hammers and ironwork of his trade.

He had close-cropped grey hair and a similarly short beard. A tightly curled coating of hair covered his body. His balls were like hens' eggs, tightly held against his body; the cock head was the same size, sitting directly on the balls. The cock head always was half way visible stretching open the foreskin. Wolf's balls were the same size, but hung low and free swinging. The cock was long, thin, and fully hidden by his thick foreskin. When relaxed the head seem to be in the middle of the skin, but fully erect, the cock remained fully sheathed.

Wolf's long foreskin had driven his mother crazy, trying to keep him from pissing on himself as a baby. Wolf's father had threatened to chop it off when he was a child, and he had lived in terror for years. He had been embarrassed and humiliated by his brothers and father. Julian saw the extra skin as having recreational potential. Julian was attracted to blond or red haired men, such as Fox, Otter and Badger, Wolf was the exception in the group.

Both of them were groggy with sleep, but Julian felt Wolf's balls and both men became alert with the potential for sexual play. He liked to stretch Wolf's ball sack and skin, trying to still further elongate them. Wolf was an unemotional, cold man, but he liked the attention Julian gave him, and especially Julian's fascination with his foreskin. He couldn't believe anyone found him attractive, not to mention his foreskin. Julian also gave him a home a regular meals, and the friendship of the other boys.

Julian quickly discovered Wolf leaked incredible amounts of pre-cum when he got excited, and since this was all trapped inside the skin, the inside of the half empty sheath was wonderfully lubricated. Julian loved the taste, and but also loved the feel of the skin as he slipped his cock in it. His thick cock and huge cock head stretched Wolf's skin to the limit, and excited both of the men. It looked as if anything else in the sheath would make it explode. In reality, there was room for both men's cum. Wolf had only joined the Harem six months earlier, and the group had only barely begun to explore the sexual potential of the man. Julian had been thinking the hairy man and his long, empty skin, might be the ideal storage place for lube and cum, that otherwise would quickly dry out.

He alone had cum in Wolf's sheath, and Julian would like to have Fox, Otter and Badger make similar deposits. Since Wolf rarely spoke, and never showed emotions, Julian was unaware he loved the attention the overlong skin was receiving.

There was a rustling. Both men became alert, straining to hear. There was silence and then another noise. They could hear a low sound, and then a repetitive sound, there was something moving through the underbrush. There was a snap, and then a thunk and a man swore. To Julian and Wolf's surprise and relief, the man swore in Latin.

I wasn't good Latin, but was street Latin, crude and vulgar. "We're lost!" a voice said.

"They must be nearby, they can't have gotten that far ahead of us," said another voice. Julian recognized something in the voice, but could not place it, but it was slightly familiar.

"I have to rest, I can't go any further!" whined the first voice. The whine clarified it all for Julian. It was the latrine attendant from the bath. "You shit eating fool!" boomed Julian. "What in hell are you doing here?"

"We mean no harm! Is that you Julian?" whined Fulvius, the attendant. By this time, all of the group was up, and had come to meet the newcomers. They were blundering through the underbrush toward Julian.

The sun had almost risen, and the forms of two men emerged. One was the small and sickly form of Fulvius, the Latrine attendant from the bath, and the second of a giant. The men knew Fulvius, of course, it had always been suspected his interest in shit was more than professional. He was always peaking at the men slyly, even though everyone in the baths was naked anyway, but no one knew the giant. Hadrian appeared, investigating the noise.

"How did you get here?" demanded Hadrian, assuming his usual leadership role. He had been the chief butler in a distinguished house was accustomed to ordering underlings about. "And who is he?" pointing to the giant.

"We were in the baths when you fled. We had nowhere to go, so we decided to flee. I thought starvation in the countryside was preferable to torture and death with the Saxons. So we ran. We saw you, and Bembo saw the Presbyter, and he figured you might know where to go," Fulvius talked quickly in a high voice. "Bembo thought we would be safe with a priest."

"And who is Bembo?"

"Bembo is a stoker in the furnace room. He works beside the hypocaust," answered Fulvius. That explained why no one had seen the man, he had been in the bowels of the public baths keeping the heating system going. Bembo just stood there saying nothing He was all but naked, with a small rag around his waist. With thick black curly hair, with a matching beard, and pale white shin, the giant obviously did not see the sun much. His body was hairless and muscular. He was built like Julian, but was a full head taller. The man was pale compared to the olive skin and deep tan of the smith.

"Bembo is my friend, I can talk to him," said Fulvius. The Presbyter understood. He alone had seen the Giant at church. Most of the men who worked in hellholes like the furnace room of the baths were dumb or afflicted some way. Bembo must be one of those poor creatures. Unlike most, he was an impressive physical specimen. "Bembo will do anything I tell him," added Fulvius.

For a group of men on the run, trying to escape from a barbarian onslaught, the latrine attendant was useless, but Bembo was an ox of a man. He was no stranger to heavy physical labor. A third bigger than any man in the group, he could be useful. Fulvius was offering himself as a translator to the dim giant. They were a pair.

No one in the group particularly wanted the latrine attendant, but everyone could see the usefulness of Bembo. Both Hadrian and Julian were eager to see under the loincloth. "Everyone pulls his own weight you know?" snarled Hadrian. "Everyone!"

"Certainly, if we could attach ourselves to such a distinguished party, you would find us to be of infinite usefulness," proclaimed the attendant. There was the look of doubt in the faces of most of the men. The sun had risen and Hadrian could clearly see the ill matched pair. Even after three days of flight, dirty, scratched and scraped, Bembo looked almost like a statue. Fulvius was downright gray; like death warned over. There was a tense silence.

The Presbyter stepped forward. "They might be a help. If they can't keep up, we can leave them." There was no enthusiastic support for the statement from the other men, but no one contradicted the official. By default, he carried the day and the two men joined the party.

The remains of the food gathered the day before was distributed. Bembo ate heartily, but Fulvius refused to eat, saying he wasn't feeling well. Julian assumed this was to reinforce his statements that he would not be a problem for the group. The ruins of the villa yielded up some treasures the looters had missed. The looters had been after treasure, but the refugees needed useful things, since they had left to old city with little more than the clothes on their backs. They soon found baskets and kitchen implements, as well as a knife.

They also found more fruits in the garden, and collected these.

It had been a half days trip from this ruined villa to the group's destination, the seaside villa. At least it had been a half day as Hadrian remembered the trip twenty years earlier in peacetime. It might be a day or two distant now.

They set off. Badger went ahead scouting. The Presbyter and Fulvius were to the rear. Bembo carried the lion's share of the materials they found in the villa, and immediately justified his inclusion in the group. You could still see the road, or more correctly the path, but it was slow going. Fulvius talked incessantly and told the Presbyter his full life story. The priest was astounded a man could spend so much time describing such an uninteresting life. He ended his story with his meeting with Bembo.

Bembo was an orphan, the product of the union between a gladiator and a whore, raised on the streets and sold to the baths at age thirteen. Fulvius had befriended him, and they had been all but inseparable for the last few years. Fulvius purported to be like a father to him, but the priest knew enough about human nature to realize fatherly feelings were not the only ones influencing Fulvius. "I fed him, I trained him. You can't look like he does on the swill they give to the stokers." A bit of fatherly pride crept into the man's voice. "He would have been dead without me."

"Of course, he took advantage of me. I was his father and his wife," added Fulvius. "But I love him so, it was all worth it." The presbyter felt he was learning more about the relationship than was desirable, but fortunately, the man decided to sit down and rest. Maximus left the man alone and joined the main group of men sitting under a tree. Hadrian said he thought the house was near, and they would get there by sundown. They all rested for a short period and Hadrian got up and started getting the group underway.

The proceeded a few hundred paces and realized Fulvius wasn't with them. Bembo and the Presbyter raced back to wake him up. They found him resting in the place they had left him, stone cold dead. "Get Magister Optimus, quickly!" Maximus ordered. Bembo ran back to the main group. Fulvius was cold, and even grayer than he had been in life.

When the group returned, the question was how to bury the man; they had no implements. Hadrian suggested they just leave him there, but there was a horrified look on Bembo's face, and Optimus then suggested they erect a pile of rocks over the body. That would protect the body from animals. Maximus said something about Celtic warrior's burials, and that seemed to calm Bembo down. It was a very rocky area, and they covered the body with a piece of cloth salvaged from the burned villa, and soon created a convincing pile of stones.

Maximus preformed the appropriate ceremonies over the pile, and the group set out again. They clearly would not get to their destination since it was already late afternoon, but no one wanted to stay by the body of the late latrine attendant. Hadrian and Fox were near the front of the line of men. "It delayed us, but it may have been a blessing in disguise, Fulvius was an unattractive character," Hadrian suggested in a low voice.

"And Bembo is the next best thing short of a horse," added Fox. "He's one impressive piece of man meat. Do you think he will find our ways congenial?"

Hadrian laughed. "Fulvius was no monk. When, ugly little monster of a man had a young Hercules fall into his lap, I can't believe it was more than a week before someone's cock was in someone's ass. And I can't believe, given Fulvius' interests, there wasn't piss and shit covering something."

"You think we may smell too good for him?" Fox laughed. "We will need to get Wolf smelling the way he did when Julian found him." Wolf had not been brought up in a Roman city, and the bath was a new experience to him. "Maybe Julian will need to retrain him. He did a great job with Wolf, and he was a hopeless case."

"I think there may be several men in the group who wouldn't mind educating the giant," Hadrian said, and he included himself in that group.

At the rear of the group, Bembo carried a heavy burden effortlessly and walked beside Maximus. "My Lord", the Giant spoke, "I'm frightened."

"Why is that?"

"Fulvius was my only protector and friend," he explained.

"I wouldn't worry about that, you are in a group of strong men," Maximus said this more to reassure himself than the giant did.

"That's not it," the giant continued, "I don't think he was a Christian. Is he in hell now?"

Maximus had encountered this situation many times before. He knew exactly what to say. "He confessed all to me, and he died at peace with the Lord." Bembo looked relieved.

A few hours later, the group stopped at dusk in a clump of trees near a small stream. They ate the remains of the food from the burned Villa, and Otter caught some fish. Bembo slept at Maximus' feet. Hadrian nudged Fox, who was on watch with him, and whispered, "I think Bembo has found his teacher."

Hadrian was worried. He had almost located the villa, but still didn't know if the original owners had re-occupied it, or if it might have become the stronghold of a Saxon chieftain. After the devastation of the burned villa, the first option seemed unlikely; the entire district was unpopulated. The second was a real possibility. Maybe he and Badger should go ahead and investigate the situation.

CHAPTER TWO

The Villa

When the group awoke the next day, Hadrian told them of his scouting plan, and all agreed it was sensible. Hadrian and Badger set off, and Julian climbed a tree to watch for danger to the north and west, Wolf to the south and east. Otter had discovered a nearby pond on his fishing expedition the day before, and the remainder of the group went with him to swim and clean up.

They stripped naked and waded into the cool water. Maximus and Optimus were upper class men who were accustomed to bathing every day. Bembo, Fox and Otter were Britons who weren't as demanding. The three men were usually under the control of their masters, but Julian was on watch, and Fulvius was dead. The Roman patricians were unused to association with common people, and didn't know what was expected. All the men, with the exception of Bembo, knew of the sexual interests of the others. All were tense and uneasy with the situation.

The cool water shriveled their balls and cocks and was too cool to stay in the water for long. They got out and lay in the sun on a grassy bank on the opposite side of the pond. Optimus sat next to

Fox. Otter joined them and sat on the other side. Maximus lay down on his stomach, and Bembo sat at his feet.

Otter and Fox looked like brothers; both were tall and thin, with blond hair. Hair covered their chests, but its pale color made it difficult to see. There was a trail of hair leading from their chests to the pubic hair, which was thick. Both had low hanging balls and long thin cocks. Otter's cock head was almost completely visible, while you could only see Fox's piss slit peaking out between the folds of foreskin.

Optimus was bald and bearded, with a surprisingly muscular body, moderate body hair and a thick and long cock. The Boys had been Julian's playmates for several years, but he kept them for himself, and they had little experience with other men. While they were inexperienced, the large equipment of the older man naturally aroused them. As the sun warmed them after the cold swim, their cocks began to respond.

Bembo was hairless except for the thick, black bush pubic area. The hair was pitch black and very long, so the cock and the balls were all but enshrouded in it. Maximus was bald, clean-shaven, but very hairy, with wavy brown chest and pubic hair. His sexual equipment was meaty, but not exceptional. It was thick rather than long. "I am stiff as a board," he said. He was lying face down in the grass, and began to stretch, much as a cat does. He stretched one arm first, then the other, then a leg. He then raised his ass in the air, stretching his back.

As his ass rose in the air, he felt something grab his ass and something brush against his asshole. Bembo was licking his asshole. He was both intensely excited and shocked. "Bembo, what are you doing?"

"You don't like it master?" asked the Giant.

"It's…," replied Maximus, he searched for words, but then surrendered to the giant's tongue. His ass was virgin, and the stimulation was different from anything he had experienced before. He moaned with pleasure.

The other three men watched with amusement and increasing excitement. Optimus saw his lover wiggle his ass to permit maximum access, just as Optimus had done many times as the priest slipped his cock into his willing ass. Fox looked at Optimus' hard cock. It grew increasingly impressive, as he got more and more excited. As the cock head emerged half way from the skin, he couldn't resist, and Fox rolled over and began licking it. The magistrate's cock was almost double the size of Julian's, and transfixed Fox who was trying to get it all in his mouth.

Otter was the odd man out, not sure either couple would welcome him. Julian tended to use them one by one rather than together. Otter couldn't decide which pair was more exciting. He stood, and saw Optimus staring at the blond man's half-erect cock. Otter dropped to his knees, straddled the man's face and fed him his cock.

Fox was a cock hound, who lived to suck, and Optimus was losing control. He was trying to eat Otter's meat, was afraid he might be too rough, but Otter just moaned. Every time he took the entire cock, Otter squirted some pre-cum into the magistrate's mouth as he pulled out. Optimus couldn't believe anything could be better, but then he felt Fox working a finger into his ass. Fox touched a magic spot and Optimus lost it. If the two men hadn't been straddling him, he would have had convulsions. His cock exploded, Fox would not let his cock escape, and Fox's rough tongue licked the ultra sensitive head as sperm flooded his mouth. Otter realized what had happened and pulled away so Optimus wouldn't choke.

Meanwhile, Bembo had replaced his tongue with his cock in Maximus' ass. Bembo's cock head was a huge mushroom on the end of a thin shaft. Once it got by the spit-lubricated sphincter, it slid in easily. An explosion of feeling immediately replaced the shock of pain. Maximus was not experienced enough to know what had happened, but Bembo's mushroom head was exactly the right size to ram Maximus' virgin prostate. Bembo hit the bull's eye on his first try.

Maximus was crying in ecstatic passion, Bembo felt his passion and instinctively pumped at the right interval for maximum penetration and watched the man melt around his cock. He could feel the ass contracting to grab hold of the cock.

Bembo had fucked Fulvius many times, but had never gotten this reaction. Fulvius' ass was like an under stuffed pillow. Maximus' ass was a sex organ, responding to every movement of Bembo's throbbing organ. Bembo shot off, drained his cock, and collapsed over the ass and back of his new lover. He felt Maximus' hard cock. It all but exploded and covered his hand and arm covered with sperm. The two men collapsed on the grass.

Otter was sitting cross-legged with Optimus' head in his lap, squeezing pre-cum from is cock and feeding it to the magistrate. Fox was still sucking the cock, draining it of every sexually generated juice.

"They are coming," cried Julian from a tree nearby.

The men returned to the water, swam to the other side and dressed. Julian had been watching from a tree overhead and had enjoyed the scene.

Hadrian and Badger's scouting expedition was both uneventful and productive. They found the villa. Sacked and partially burned, it had never been re-occupied. There was no sign anyone had been in the place recently. They all set off and were at the villa by noon.

Optimus and Maximus were unimpressed. It had been pleasant enough house and either would have been satisfied with it as their own property, but it was by no means impressive. Why Hadrian had been so impressed was unclear to them. The others were perfectly satisfied.

Hadrian showed them around the charred ruins with pride and pleasure. Attached to the house as a boy, he remembered many happy hours there. The owners built it into the side of a cliff overlooking the Atlantic. The outer rooms had been grand and elaborate, but as the men followed Hadrian deeper into the house, the rooms became darker and smaller. They weren't luxurious at all.

In the innermost room, a fine fresco remained in an elaborate frame. The picture was of Jupiter raping Ganymede and, unlike most depictions of that scene, it left nothing to the imagination. Jupiter had a cock more suited for a satyr or Bacchus. Ganymede was obviously trying to open his ass cheeks wide enough to accommodate the huge member. The divine cock was actually three-dimensional and emerged from the stucco wall.

Hadrian walked up the plaster cock, pretended to jerk it off, and the panel swung open. There was a room beyond. The space was dark, but you could see a glimmer of light in the deep recess. Hadrian led the men into the dark space. For about ten paces, the passage was narrow, but it began to widen, and actually get lighter. There was a bend, the brightness dramatically increased. Suddenly, there was a broad, domed rotunda, illuminated by sunlight pouring through an oculus above. On each side were other chambers, and the sound of running water.

Hadrian said, "To the left is a thermal spring forming a caldarium. To the right is a cold plunge, the frigidarium. This is a natural bath." The rooms were bright only by comparison to the dark passage that served them. As the men's eyes adapted to the light level, the extraordinary decoration of the rooms became clearer. It was all male erotica, pornography. Mosaic and frescoed representations of every possible sexual act covered the walls and ceiling. Excluded from the murals only were any acts requiring a woman's participation.

"In here we are hidden from the world, safe from view and attack. The door can be sealed and we are safe!" Hadrian proclaimed. The combination of physical safety and intense lust made him almost giddy. "Badger and I checked the mechanism of the door, and it still works. We can close our self in and be protected for days."

"Can't the Barbarians see the villa?" Julian asked.

"Sure they can," Hadrian answered, "but the thermal spring gives off steam and mist. This outcropping of stone marks a treacherous part of the coastline. My Master called it the Point of the Mists and anyone who knows the coast knows to steer away from the dangers below. The villa was sacked in a slave uprising, not by the Saxons."

The thermal spring warmed the room. The men began to assimilate the beauty and convenience of the space. An underground chamber with natural light, heat and water was very appealing, especially since it was almost invisible from outside.

"It's time for a bath," cried Julian. Everyone striped and proceeded to the two bathing chambers. Julian, who had been watching the earlier sexual play from his treetop, noted the men seemed to be much more comfortable than they had been. Hadrian noted the change too, but didn't know what had brought about the change. At first Julian wanted to punish the boys for playing with other men, but he had been so excited by what he had seen, be decided to see how they responded to being sexual toys for the other men in the group.

Julian didn't admit even to himself he felt a itching in his ass as he watched Optimus' cock reach full erection. His annoyance with Fox was because he had hidden this huge instrument in his mouth. He didn't want to admit he was more than curious to find out whether cock size played a role in sexual pleasure.

Hadrian had very firm thoughts on the subject of cock size; he had tried big ones and loved them. The prospect of multiple partners excited him. He could suck, or fuck, or be fucked for half a day or more, but he wore out his partners. He wanted many men who were willing to play and force him endure a marathon of sexual contact.

As the empire collapsed, women disappeared. They were raped, starved and frozen in the harsh new reality, although, nothing equaled the danger of childbirth. Women were ephemeral things, and few might last long enough to produce a child and then die. Men were everywhere, actually only strong men. The weak ones were dead. They were strong men with strong sexual desires and they had nowhere to deposit their man juices, nowhere to work off their energy.

Hadrian had been on a long sea voyage once and discovered the truth about men. Filled with sexual drive and energy, they often had no sexual outlet. Alone on a ship with no companions but men, after a night of drinking, the captain would fuck every man on the boat. This Hadrian had expected. As the final event of the night, the captain opened his ass and the crew fucked him. The captain was still begging for more after the last man filled his ass. Hadrian rose to fill the captain's needs. Hadrian had never felt such a tender and delicate ass, filled with the seed of a score of men. Hadrian's cock was average in size, but he had incredible stamina, and he fucked for half the night, the captain was whimpering for him to stop as the sun rose. Both he and the captain passed out.

When the captain woke, it was as if nothing had happened. Everyone seemed to have forgotten the events of the previous night. The Captain was the same aggressive bastard he was before. His attitude towards Hadrian had changed though; he knew a man with special skills when he found one. The same orgy occurred several times again. Near the end of the voyage after the men had filled the Captain's ass and passed out, Hadrian was pumping the captain's ass. He quietly talked with the captain. "Do they really not remember?" Hadrian asked.

"Shit," answered the Captain. "Some of us have been doing this for five or ten years, as long as we've been together. They think it gives them strength. I shoot my seed into their guts; I take theirs. It makes us family." The Captain was trying to keep Hadrian's cock out of his ass by squeezing tight. With all the crews' cum lubricating the hole, this was impossible, but the feeling was good for both men.

"I hope I wasn't intruding."

"Hell no! I like a little variety," continued the Captain. "You should be on a ship when we have a new man. The men go wild with the prospect of a virgin ass. They work him over good, and then I do the final stretching exercises." The captain was a big man, so Hadrian knew what he meant. "Sometimes the guy is a bit worn and ripped by the time we are done. Let me tell you, when he gets his cock in my ass for the first time, he thinks he has died and gone to heaven. He feels my warm tunnel, I squeeze him with my sphincter, and milk him a bit; he is the emperor in Rome! It works every time." Hadrian maintained a steady rhythm, as the Captain demonstrated his technique.

"I would be glad to join in," Hadrian volunteered.

"You must be a part of the crew," the Captain answered seriously. "On the ship we need to travel light, so the cock and the nut inside our ass is the only plaything we have. I use them for brotherhood, not recreation." Hadrian planned to fuck him until dawn, but his body had different intentions, his rhythm quickened and his cock head became more and more sensitive. The Captain noticed the change. By unspoken agreement, they pushed to a climax.

Hadrian's seed merged with the sailors, and the captain shot a remarkable load for a man who had cum many times that night.

Hadrian kept the captain's legs in the air, knelt down, and licked the Captain's tender ass. The captain moaned, Hadrian said, "If the sailors can't fuck me, at least I can taste their seed." The Captain understood what Hadrian wanted, relaxed his ass and let some of the juice escape. Hadrian licked until dawn, as small amounts of man seed dribbled from the captain's ass.

Hadrian had dreamed about this experience for years, and hoped this group of men might be the opportunity to turn his dream into reality.

Hadrian and Julian were on watch that night. "Tell me about the Boys." Hadrian had not been alone with Julian for a year or so, and his curiosity had built. When the men had been close they told everything to each other, and Julian reverted to this pattern.

"I found Fox first. He had been in some sort of trouble on the Saxon shore and had escaped west. I think he was escaping from creditors. He didn't seem to have any skills for making his way in the world, and was hungry and I took him in, for a night and a quick fuck I thought.

"I fed him, took him to the baths and cleaned him up, and returned to my house for fun and games. I planned to fuck him for the night, but made him suck my cock first. He was very unwilling, which I liked. You remember I like to make men do what I want, and since I was so much stronger than he was, I anticipated a pleasant struggle.

"I finally got his mouth to my cock and he took it in. I was a little worried he might bite, but he was in my control, and could have guessed the consequences. There was no need to worry. Fox later told me it was the first time he had sucked cock, and he loved it. He couldn't get enough of it, and he was good. He's a natural cocksucker, born to have a cock in his throat.

"I lay down and let him go to work. You're good Hadrian, but Fox is a master. I shot off, he kept sucking, I shot again, and he still sucked. It was as if he had attached himself to my cock. I woke in the morning and he was still there, asleep with my cock in his mouth. I decided to keep him. You don't find a man with his need to suck often. I figured I could rent him out for parties. After a week, I got to like him. I like him a lot. You didn't even need to pay him, as long as he got a few loads of cum a week fresh from my cock.

"A few months later Otter arrived. He needed work, and a place to stay, no questions asked. I had gotten used to blond men and liked them. He fit the bill, and looked strong, even if he was thin. He did what he was told and slept on the floor next to the bed. He didn't seem to mind Fox and me playing. One night Fox broke off his sucking to heed the call of nature, and when he returned, he found Otter skewered on my cock.

"Otter's ass was small, and it was the tightest fit I have ever felt. Otter sat his hole on the spit-lubricated cock and just sat down, one movement, no sign of pain. Fox came back, disappointed. I made him wait until the next day to suck again. He was mad, but the next time he sucked me he was even better. They got into a contest, was I happier being sucked by Fox or fucking Otter? I never let them play with each other, only me."

"It must have been a year later when Badger arrived at my shop. He looked like a smaller version of the other boys, more muscular, and with a bigger cock. He had no objections to our living arrangements. He fit right in. I like the taste of his cock, and he mine." Julian concluded.

"Don't they get jealous?" Hadrian asked.

"Not really, Fox was a bit uneasy at first, but excited later, he likes the thought of sucking a cock that had been in his rival's ass. Badger is so affable, everyone gets along with him, and doesn't seem to think of him as a rival," Julian answered. "I never let them play together, but they seem to be willing to experiment." He then told Hadrian about the scene by the pond.

"Pandora's box has been opened!" Hadrian exclaimed. "And the prospects are exciting. You are going to share the Boys?"

"I guess I need to if I am going to be able to sample the rest of the meat in the group," Julian answered. "I have never been in a group where everyone shares my lusts. There doesn't seem to be anyone who doesn't play. For the first time in my life I don't need to hide my interests."

Hadrian thought back to his experience on the ship. There the enjoyment could only occur in the dark after everyone was drunk. The Villa presented a different prospect, a prospect Hadrian found attractive. A prospect he guessed everyone would find attractive too.

"It's odd, but given everyone in the group shares common sexual interests, most are relatively inexperienced," observed Hadrian. "Present company excluded, of course."

Julian smiled. "You're lucky your ass hasn't closed up with calluses! Half the dirty, filthy, degrading and incredibly enjoyable acts that make up my sex life I learned from you."

"You aren't telling me you weren't ready for my lessons!" Hadrian said. "I may have been the first person to touch your hole since your mother taught you how to wipe your ass, but you certainly knew how to open up wide. Shit, Hannibal could have driven his army and his elephants into your ass, and you'd have been ready."

"Well, it looks to me we may have some teaching to do. And I think we have some willing students," Julian remarked.

Inside the cave, the other men decided to try the hot baths; they walked naked into the warm room. The pool was five paces wide, domed, and warm with a sight smell of sulfur in the air. It was quite dark as the only light came from the door to the bigger central room. You could see the men next to you, but not those on the other side of the pool. The men didn't know the room, and they stepped in carefully. There was a step to a platform forming a good seat on the edge. The center of the pool was deep. When Wolf realized this, he dove in and swam across the pool in the bubbly warm water.

All of the men felt safe for the first time in days when they closed and secured the outer door of the underground villa. Everyone relaxed as they sank into the warm water in the darken room. After a short while, the tenseness seemed to leave their bodies. They relaxed, their balls hung lower, and old urges emerged. Maximus sat next to Fox and longed to be alone, so that he could seduce the man.

He suddenly realized everyone in the group shared his interests, and that was no reason to avoid contact. He reached over and touched Fox, who moved closer. Fox reached to touch Maximus, and felt for his cock. It was already erect. The pulled closer together.

Fox stood up, raised Maximus so he was sitting on the edge of the pool and swallowed the Presbyter's cock in one movement. The tangled blond hair and the droopy mustache of the Briton draped over Maximus' meat. Maximus lay out stretched parallel to the edge of the pool, Fox had one foot in the pool, and raised the other on the side. Bembo sat next to the pair, and saw Fox's asshole, stretched wide open. It reminded him of Fulvius. This had been his favorite position, so Bembo decided to accept the invitation presented by the asshole

The sudden contact between his hole and a cock head offended Fox, but when Maximus saw the giant approach, and realized his intentions. His cock filled with pre-cum and flooded Fox's mouth with the sticky fluid. The seamen intoxicated Fox; he couldn't think of anything but the cock in his mouth. As Bembo's huge mushroom entered the ass there was a burst of pain, then relief as the hole returned to a more normal diameter and the shaft entered.

No one had fucked Fox before. Fox thought this wasn't too bad. He continued to suck Maximus as Bembo slowly pulsed his cock into his tight ass. Maximus was dribbling a constant stream of pre-cum; this kept Fox sucking.

Fox could suck for hours, and was settling in for a long session, when he began to feel a warm, intensely sexual feeling spreading from inside his ass. Bembo was a bit disappointed, Fox's ass was tight, but not the responsive sexual organ Maximus was. Badger floated across the pool on his back and positioned his head under Fox's engorged cock. He took it in his mouth.

The feelings were almost too much for Fox; while he wanted to break away to cool off and calm down, but the steady stream, now almost a river, of pre-cum glued him the Maximus' cock. He was feeling extraordinary sensations emanating from his mouth, cock and ass. Bembo was the first to notice the change in Fox. He was twitching, and clenching his ass around Bembo's pulsing cock. Bembo pick up speed. Badger felt the new rhythm and tasted Fox's pre-cum for the first time.

"He's going to pop!" yelled Bembo. Fox was involuntarily twitching now; Badger's mouth filled with what seemed like buckets of cum. Fox's orgasm pushed both Maximus and Bembo over the edge. Bembo and Maximus shot their seed into the man from his ass and mouth. Badger alone kept his load. The other men collapsed into the pool. Maximus cradled Fox in his arms, and Fox wept. Fox hadn't known the feelings were in him, the sexual ecstasy. He couldn't believe the feelings, and suspected they were perhaps unmanly.

That night Maximus, Fox and Bembo slept together.

Wolf sat next to Optimus and Otter on the other side of the pool. Wolf was a loner, and wasn't prone to talk. He was naturally taciturn, and the cultured magistrate who sat next to him amplified this characteristic. He had never spoken to a man of rank before. Wolf liked the darkness and the water because it obscured his cock and the overly long tube of skin that was a source of so much embarrassment to him.

Otter was, by contrast, naturally gregarious, and soon had an active conversation with Optimus. He was also naturally aggressive, and had the magistrate's cock at full attention in no time at all. Otter whispered into Optimus' ear, "Feel out Wolf's meat; it's a wonder." Optimus obeyed.

The warm water relaxed all of the men's genitals, with the ball sack dropping and the cock lengthening. As Optimus felt, it seemed as if Wolf's balls were a foot's length from his body, and the cock seemed impossibly long. Optimus was impressed and excited. "Beautiful!" he whispered into Wolf's ear. "Just beautiful"

Wolf, who has tensed up with the contact, relaxed. He had been afraid Julian was the only man to find his equipment attractive. Now there were two. His cock responded. At this point Badger swam back from the other side of the pool when Fox had just exploded. He bumped into Optimus, who got up and sat on the edge of the pool.

In the dim light Badger could see the magistrate's erection, and he licked the balls dangling below it. He figured the men had been playing, so he extended his arms and snagged Otter and Wolf's erections. He took a firm grip on each, using the cocks as support for his assault on Optimus' cock. He was floating on the water, supported by cock in each hand and the third in his mouth.

As he pulled down on the cocks, he would rise from the water and get a good taste of Optimus while he jerked the other men. Optimus pulled the two men closer, with his arms around their shoulders and Badger took care of all three. Badger was a good judge of sexual excitement and he realized all the men were at the same level, and they might climax together. Wolf moaned. Badger's mouth filled with Optimus' sperm and felt the involuntary pulsing of Wolf and Otter's cocks as the shot their loads into the water.

Badger was the only man in the group to have balls still filled with seed. He wondered how long he could keep it. He was tremendously excited, but didn't want to shoot. He wanted the juice to build up in his cock, to ripen and fill every available space in his cock, so when he did shoot, it would be a marvel.

CHAPTER THREE

Storm

All the men were natives of interior areas of Britain, and were surprised at the violence of the storms that battered the coastline. Normally days were filled with work, but nothing could be done in the driving rains and violent winds of these storms. The men took refuge in the cave and relaxed. The skylights provided good light in the rooms, and the men could see each other well. The men stripped for a trip to the baths; Hadrian had bound his cock in a rawhide tie.

"I'm exhausted!" exclaimed Optimus.

"I'm horny enough to fuck a horse!" countered Julian. Julian walked over to Badger and picked him up. He turned Badger upside down and then took the diminutive man's over sized cock in his mouth. Badger's head dangled below until he caught Julian's foreskin and sucked it in his mouth. The speed of the movement caught all the men off guard. The Boys had seen Julian do this many times before, but the other men were pleasantly shocked.

"I thought you wanted to fuck!" Hadrian cried. Julian wanted to reply, but Badger's cock was fully erect and fully penetrated his throat. He couldn't say a word. He also could not breathe. Julian choked.

Bembo came over, grabbed Badger's legs and lifted him straight up, letting air into Julian's throat and freeing Julian's cock from the sucking mouth. He then turned Badger around and took the engorged member into his own mouth. Badger obediently used his tongue to search Bembo's bush for a cock head and soon had it. Badger lips held on to the cock head while his tongue located the piss slit.

The men watched and laughed at the comic, but lusty display. Hadrian went from man to man binding each man's cock in a rawhide thong. This day off from work would last.

"Julian needs a smaller cock!" Hadrian joked. "Optimus, can you help him out?" The butler knew Julian liked to dominate, and knew he wanted to try Optimus' cock, the biggest organ in the group. He also wondered whether the desire to dominate or the lust for cock would triumph in Julian's mind.

The scene greatly excited Optimus and broke through his normal reserve. He walked over to Julian and offered him his dick. Julian took one lick and then greedily attacked the cock. It was only half-erect, but Julian quickly manipulated it into full erection. Julian's cock head, which had withdrawn into the foreskin when he choked, now re-emerged, shinny and purple red. Hadrian laughed. He had guessed lust and curiosity would triumph over reserve and the desire to control.

All the men were erect now and with their bound cocks felt a need for sexual release. Bembo carefully lowered Badger to the floor and they resumed mutual sucking. Maximus joined them taking Badger's meaty balls into his mouth. Bembo glanced up with Badger's cock still in his mouth and saw Maximus. Maximus kissed Bembo's forehead and returned to Badger's ball sack. Bembo was relieved his new master approved of his new playmate. Badger was having a hard time dealing the waves of feeling coming from his cock and balls, as well as the taste of Bembo's cock. It had spurted pre-cum when the second man began to lick Badger's balls. His cock continued to leak badly.

Optimus was trying to get his entire cock into Julian's mouth without much success. Julian was working on it, but not making much headway. Wolf approached Optimus and opened his foreskin in Optimus' face. Optimus stuck out his tongue and Wolf let it enter the empty skin. Hadrian sensed it was a new feeling for the magistrate. The tight warm skin contracted on the tongue and as Optimus sucked the skin into his mouth as he forced his tongue deeper into the skin. His tongue tasted the rich brew of precum. The enveloping foreskin had stored the cock juices and they were ripe. A few seconds later Optimus tasted fresh pre-cum, and lots of it. A second later the tongue licked Wolf's cock head.

With Optimus' tongue completely enveloped in the skin, he soon located Wolf's piss slit and then pushed deeper to encircle the head. The head was oval and a bit pointed; it was a tight fit. It took effort to force his tongue past the swollen head into the deeper recesses of the foreskin. When he probed as far as he could he licked the ultra sensitive edge of the head and the cock responded to the tongue by twitching.

Wolf's entire body twitched when the rough tongue flicked where a thin membrane of skin connected the head to the foreskin. Like everything else about Wolf, this was long. Optimus encountered a strong musky taste in the two recesses on each side of the membrane. He went after both of these with vigor, curiously excited by the taste. Wolf twitched as the tongue caressed the underside of the head, and began to growl. Hadrian stood behind Wolf, caressing his tits, and rubbing his erect cock in Wolf's hairy ass crack. By now, Fox was sucking Julian's cock, but Optimus didn't know this, since he was looking the other way. He was only playing with Wolf's cock head, and he could only see the thick tangled hairs of Wolf's pubic bush; Optimus realized Wolf had a long cock. Optimus did notice Julian was had given up on getting the cock in his mouth, and was sucking the magistrate's equally large balls, and licking his asshole.

Optimus pulled his tongue back to taste the juice from Wolf's piss slit, then darted it back into the recesses on the underside of the engorged cock. It was a tighter fit than before and Optimus realizes Wolf was even more excited. The foreskin stretched as thin as possible to contain his throbbing cockhead, and the magistrate's entire tongue.

Hadrian' cock was at full erection, his head clear of the skin and covered in pre-cum which he was using to coat Wolf's ass. He felt Wolf's twitching, and heard the deep growling that was emanating from the excited man. Hadrian was equally excited and decided to push him over the edge. He nuzzled his pre-cum covered cock head at Wolf's ass ring, not penetrating, just knocking at the door. Wolf bellowed as he shot off.

His cock exploded, filling up every space between the skin, the cock and the tongue. Optimus' tongue was awash in Wolf's man juice. Every time Wolf shot a load of cream, Optimus tongue caressed the underside of the trapped cock.

Hadrian felt each of Wolf's convulsive shudders and Hadrian shot his load and showered Wolf's asshole with sperm. Hadrian thought he detected Wolf opening his ass a bit, as the hole was drenched; he saved this information for later use.

Eventually, Optimus withdrew his tongue, and Wolf collapsed on the floor, into Hadrian' arms. Hadrian hugged the man, rubbed his furry chest and helped him calm down from the sexual high. Wolf was drained and limp. Hadrian then took his limp cock and worked his tongue into the contracting skin, and cleaned up the remains cum and saliva inside the shaft. Wolf's twitching diminished, as Hadrian slowly explored the inside of his foreskin. Only when Hadrian licked he tender underside of the head did Wolf convulse again and shoot, a larger gob of cum. Hadrian didn't mind eating others' cum, as he had discovered on the ship years ago, but he did appreciate it when it was fresh. He thought of it as a tribute to his sexual skills.

Julian thought he was done. Fox had sucked his cock to a good erection, and had begun to eat his asshole, covering the opening with spit. Optimus rose, and Julian could breathe again, but Optimus had not climaxed. He wanted to fuck. Optimus was a natural bottom, but his bound cock was rock hard, and needed release. The blacksmith was an impressive man, and his muscular ass gave promise of being tight.

"If you can't take it in your mouth, let's see if it fits in your ass," Optimus suggested. Fox had Julian's legs in the air so he could eat his ass, and Julian was effectively pinned to the floor. Otter came over. He loved a cock in his ass and hoped Optimus member would fill him up. Optimus told him to give some advice to Julian. Otter held Julian's legs and fingered the smith's hole. Fox spit on the ass and then Fox sucked Optimus and left the monster cock dripping with saliva. Fox had no problem sucking and breathing

Optimus vaguely planned to enter Julian's ass slowly and work his way up his chute, but as soon as his cock head cleared the sphincter, he plunged deep and his pubic hairs were intermingled with Julian's ass hairs. Julian bellowed, and screamed, "You're ripping me in half! You're killing me!"

Optimus was enjoying the hot tunnel too much to care. It was tight, completely enveloping his cock with no room to spare. He felt the smith's ass was molding itself to the shape of his monster member as he pushed it pulsed in and pulled it out. Julian continued to yell and scream, but Optimus saw Julian's cock had, if anything, grown harder, and Julian was wiggling his ass to get a better position. Optimus slowed down his pounding. Julian quieted down. Optimus leaned over the smith, stretched his legs further back, opened the ass wider, and looked Julian in the face. Julian whispered, "Pull out and go in again, a bit slower. I've got to catch my breath." Optimus complied.

Otter and Fox, who had been enjoying the scene, went back to work; Otter re-lubricated Julian's ass, and Fox sucked Optimus' cock. The taste of pre-cum was everywhere on the member, and Otter had to pull him away when Optimus indicated he wanted to go in again. Fox and Otter watched as Optimus popped his cock head through the sphincter muscle five or six times before going deep in a slow but continuous movement. It was clear Optimus' cock woke Julian's prostate. Julian just moaned this time.

Fox positioned his balls over Julian's mouth, leaned forward and sucked the smith's cock. He had a wonderful view of the cock slowing pumping into the ass, and tasted Julian as he oozed globs of pre-cum every time Optimus penetrated deeply. Otter watched from the back. The magistrate's low hanging, big balls made it difficult to see the cock plug the ass, but Otter noticed Optimus was spreading Julian's legs, to increase the tightness on the cock, exposing his asshole. Otter licked a few fingers and toyed with Optimus' ass. He found the prostate, and Optimus reacted like a horse at the racetrack, released at the starting line. He was pumping wildly, Julian was bucking, and Fox was trying to hold him still as the pre-cum flowed. Gushing man juice soon replaced the sweet precum. Otter felt the sponge like nut in Optimus' ass turn hard as a rock, and saw him arch his back and stare at the ceiling as he filled the quivering body of the blacksmith with his sperm.

Optimus and Julian climaxed together, synchronized with Julian's cock shooting long ribbons of cum across his hairy gut and chest as Optimus plunged deep depositing his load in the innermost recesses of the blacksmiths rectum. Optimus collapsed on Julian, smearing the seed on their chests as they kissed, but still leaving his cock firmly enveloped in Julian's ass.

Fox and Otter then turned their attention to Maximus, Badger and Bembo. By this time, Bembo had his cock in Maximus' ass. Maximus was on his back on a raised platform on the side of the room. His cock stood straight up pointing to the ceiling. Otter quickly saw the potential, and jumped on the platform, straddled the Presbyter and positioned his asshole above the cock. Otter lowered his ass and glowed with relief as the cock filled his hole.

Otter was a fuck slut, his hole and prostate were ultra sensitive and as soon as a cock touched, or entered it he felt waves of sexual passion. He positioned himself for maximum stimulation. He spread his legs wide on each side of Maximus; his knees all but touched his shoulders as he tried to open as wide as he could for the throbbing cock. He used the cock to balance himself as he raised and lowered his ass. He was bumping into Bembo as they both used Maximus.

Badger guided him so when Bembo plunged deep into Maximus' ass Otter raised so the only the cock head was in his ass. As Bembo pulled out, Badger pushed Otter down so he was fully impaled. Fox straddled Maximus face the leaned forward to suck

Otter's cock. Briefly, the rhythm was perfect, and all four men were fully involved sexually. It could only last for a short while.

Maximus popped first, shooting his load into Otter's hot ass. Bembo felt his spasms and shot next. Otter almost lost his balance when Bembo broke the rhythm and gave the quick thrusts that put him over the edge. Maximus' still spewing cock popped out of Otter's ass, and Otter had a look of deep disappointment. Badger grabbed him, kept Otter from falling, pulled him to the side and buried his cock in Otter's just vacated ass.

Julian claimed Badger was more cock than man. While his meat was a bit smaller than Optimus', in proportion to his diminutive body it was huge. Optimus stretched Otter's cum filled ass to its limit and Otter all but shot off. Fox had been left cock less, when Otter all but fell off Maximus' cock. He was rewarded by seeing a huge gob or pre-cum emerge from Otter's cock just as Badger plowed him. Like a loadstone pointing north, he was on Otter's prick.

Once the shock of Badger's cock ramming Otter's prostate diminished, Otter calmed down and settled in for a long fuck. He had never been fucked by Badger before, and never been fucked by a cock the size of Badger's. Otter instinctively knew Badger had stamina. His hole was completely filled, normally he would try to massage the engorged penis, but that was not possible. He was an active bottom, but with Badger up his ass, he had nothing to do but let nature take its course and enjoy the sensations radiating from his ass. He was briefly worried Fox might push him over the edge, but Fox was just staring at his cock head and licking up the beads of pre-cum that emerged.

Badger began to speed up his ramming, and Otter realized it would be over shortly. Fox suddenly deep throated Otter's cock and tasted the first spurt of man seed. Badger felt a spot in Otter's ass a get harder and harder; it rubbed against the underside of his cock and he began to fuck frantically. He shot half his load in Badger's ass, then pulled out when his cock head got too sensitive to stand the friction of the tight ass. He shot over Otter and his seed landed on Fox.

Everyone climaxed except for Fox who still wanted to suck. Everyone was relaxed, and a bit sleepy. They went to the thermal spring and bathed. The storm continued to rage outside, they all ate some dinner and night fell. Hadrian and Julian were on the first watch. They wrapped themselves in animal skins and went outside.

"My ass will be sore for a month!" complained Julian.

"You faker! You used to take my cock without complaint. Be a man!" the unsympathetic Hadrian replied, "You know I would gladly have taken your place. And put on a better show!"

"Your cock and Optimus' donkey dong are not related, I am not sure what you have is even worthy of being considered a cock!" Julian said. "Shit, it ripped me apart. It hurt."

"You mean it hurt at first."

"Yah, it hurt at first. I got used to it really fast. I was never so surprised in my life when he buried it in my ass in one movement, I was sure a patrician like him would have eased it in. He found something deep in there I didn't know was there," said Julian. "I thought most of my insides were trying to squeeze the cock out of my ass. I am afraid the boys will never look at me the same."

"The boys seem to enjoy the view," observed Hadrian, "I think men like to know what a man can take. They don't mind seeing you in sexual ecstasy, shooting your guts out of your cock. They were excited. I am afraid," he added," you had better get used to having a lot more cum in your ass than you have had in the last few years."

"I can still feel that donkey dick churning up my insides. That man is a natural fucker. Once he calmed down, he really seemed to know what I liked. If I twitched, he would work his cock into the same place and pound it three of four more times, then pull out just as I was beginning to get too hot. He'd poke around a few more places until I twitched again. I'd love to see what Otter would do skewered on that pole!" Julian said.

"Did anyone else fuck Otter, other than you?"

"I don't think so, at least not while he was with me. Tell me, what did you think of Wolf?" asked Julian. "He's an odd one."

"That cock of his must be the eighth wonder of the world. I have never seen a cock like his. His cum inside his skin was just as fresh as when he shot it," answered Hadrian. "He was happy enough having me explore it. I don't know what Optimus did with him, but he was awfully relaxed by the time I got to play with him. He's a crude looking man, but seems to have warmed up to us and our games."

Julian told Hadrian Wolf's history and his own scheme for fully exploiting the recreational potential of Wolf's foreskin.

"What's that? There is something out there!" Hadrian pointed to a dark spot on the sea in the distance. They were on the main terrace of the ruined villa, overlooking the stormy sea. The fierce breakers crashed in the rocks at the base of the cliff the house sat on. The two men weren't sure they saw anything, but the realized that in the constantly shifting sea, there was a recurring dark spot. "Go in and get the others," ordered Julian. Hadrian ran through the villa and to the concealed door.

They all gathered, getting their makeshift weapons, and watched the spot get closer. "If it's a ship it's doomed," Hadrian said, "It's being driven into the rocks, the currents in this area are treacherous and once you are caught there is no way to escape."

Just as the spot was close enough to make it clear it was a ship, it broke in half. "Lucky, praise the Lord!" exclaimed the Presbyter, "It was a Saxon ship. I recognize the shape."

"Was it a war party or just a ship caught in the storm?" asked Optimus.

"It makes no difference to us. They're all dead now," answered the always-sensible Julian. "All the same, we had better check the shore tomorrow and make sure they are all dead." The men decided to double the guard for the night. They would see what was left the next day.

The day dawned bright and clear, a bit cool, but comfortable. The men climbed down to the edge of the water. There was no beach directly below the villa, only rocks, but there was some on each side of the immediate area. Julian took the Boys to search the area to the west; the remainder of the men went east. Julian found several bodies dressed in Saxon garb, but badly beaten up. The rocks had done their work on those men. One of the bodies still carried his sword and had an impressive broach. They striped the body and threw it back into the sea.

To the east there were three more bodies. Maximus was the first to see the shattered remains of the stern of the ship. The tide was out and it stood on a broad sandy beach. There was a moan. Bembo and Optimus were both armed; Optimus had a sword, Bembo a club. They move up on the wreck carefully. The sound of the surf was loud enough to make it possible to sneak up on the remains of the ship.

They raised their weapons as they circled to the front of the shattered wooden hull. There were two men chained to the hull, naked with their arms and legs bleeding where the metal shackles cut into their skin. They were mumbling "Pater Noster in ceilo…"

"My God they are Christian!" exclaimed Maximus.

"Are you Romans?" one of the men asked.

"Yes Romans," Maximus answered. He realized they had found Roman prisoners, saved only because their chains didn't allow them to be swept into the sea. One of the men looked at them in astonishment and then passed out. Bembo and Optimus set about trying to free the two prisoners, but soon decided to send Hadrian to get Julian. The needed a blacksmith. Optimus and Maximus revived the men, gave them water and tried to dress the wounds. There was a stream nearby and they were able to clean the cuts, and the clear water stopped the stinging of the salt water in the ripped skin.

Optimus noticed first the men were almost identical and then he saw the men had no foreskins. Their cock heads were exposed to view. More remarkably, each man had a thick gold ring inserted through his piss slit. The magistrate took hold of the ring, and shook it and the cock. The man didn't react in pain. The man looked Optimus in the eye and said, "You noticed it?"

"I certainly did! What is it? What happened?" asked Optimus. The man didn't seem to mind having Optimus fondle his golden ring, so Optimus continued to play.

"I will tell you all about it later," answered the man who then closed his eyes too tired to talk.

Julian arrived and made short work of the chains. They carried the two men up the cliff, and decided to take them into the subterranean villa. The gold rings fascinated all of the men. The two prisoners were young, attractive, tall and thin, with a mat of chest hair connected to the pubic hair by a thin line of hair. Their cocks were long and thin. They ate, bathed and went to sleep. During the night, one of the men woke and listened to the activity in the darkness. He recognized the sounds of man sex, and he fell back to sleep, relieved he and his friend had fallen into congenial company.

The next day the two men felt much better and Optimus applied new herbs to the wounds. Most of the men left to continue the search of the beach. They weren't looking for survivors. They were looking for loot. Fox and Hadrian stayed with the former prisoners whose names were Theodosius and Marcus. The cut cocks and rings fascinated Fox. While Hadrian searched to find some sort of clothes for the naked men, Fox talked with the men, and touched the rings. As Optimus had told Fox, they didn't seem to mind having their cocks fondled. When Hadrian returned, he discovered the two men didn't mind having their cocks sucked either. Something about the way he acted suggested this was not a new experience for the them.

That night Optimus asked them to tell their story.

"I am Theodosius and this is Marcus; we are twins," he said glancing toward the other man. "We are Romans from Hispania. We were on a voyage to Britannia and were captured by pirates about five years ago, and eventually sold to a tribal chieftain in the far north of Germania. The chieftain, Othacar, seemed to like us and he decided to mark us as his own. He was a big bear of a man, and liked young men. He had no interest in boys. We were fifteen then with beards growing and hair beginning to appear on our chests and we were used in the chief's steam house. We were circumcised so we could be identified as slaves in the baths." Optimus sat next to Theodosius and was fondling the young man's cock, which was beginning to rise. Optimus realized what he meant when he said the chieftain liked them.

"The chieftain and his men enjoyed us, but could swing from great affection to cruelty. The idea of Roman twins seems to attract him for what reason we did not know... until later. When they circumcised us they all got very drunk pulled out an ax and chopped the skin off." Wolf looked horror-stricken; Julian had an erection.

"We thought they were going to castrate us, but it was just the skins they removed. The tribal wise man applied herbs and tied off the bloody remains. Othacar took the severed skins and stretched them over his cock, and wore them as a ring for a week. He was very kind to us and concerned we would heal quickly. He also wanted us to watch him play with his cock, and climax while his cock was still ringed by our foreskins."

"Half a year later the rings came," Theodosius continued, "It started with a small ring, and incredible pain. After that, every two months, a new, larger ring was worked into the hole. Eventually Othacar inserted the gold ring and we were his."

"Did it still hurt? When they enlarged the hole?" Maximus asked.

"I hate to tell you this, but as the rings got bigger, it got more and more stimulating. It was difficult to get a new ring in without an erection. Othacar and his men got drunk every time they added a new ring. They got more and more excited. The ring changes occurred at the full moon, and the entire mood of the steam house changed. When they circumcised us one man, Athgar, had an erection, by the time the gold ring was inserted, everyone in the room was erect and sucking or fucking," Theodosius continued the story.

"After we learned their language the wise man of the tribe told us the chieftain was selected by the size of his cock. They thought the biggest man was the most powerful and strongest." Optimus cast a quick look to Badger. They understood each other. "Othacar was a big man. It seemed any man in his presence who got erect, was his playmate for the night. I never saw anything like the way Othacar buried his cock in Athgar's ass. It was spectacular." There was a trace of admiration in Theodosius' voice.

"Marcus and I were dreading the time when Othacar would screw us, but we didn't know if the chieftain's penis was reserved for his men, and forbidden to slaves. We figured it could only be so bad, after having part of our cocks chopped off and metal rings forced thought our cock heads. All the men would play with our cocks, but never our ass holes. No mouth touched our cocks…except for Othacar, of course."

"The wise man told us the tribal god was called Twin Odin, the double blessed. He had four legs, four arms, two heads, and two cocks. We saw the statue, and felt a longing for Roman art. It was crude and poorly made, every bit a barbarians work. The only part of the statue the sculptor, if sculptor you could call him, showed any skill was in his depiction of two, large and lifelike cocks."

"It seems the chieftains of tribe were in power for only ten years, after that time they would be sacrificed to Twin Oden and a new horse hung leader selected. The only way Othacar could survive would be to be fucked by Twin Oden, who would refresh the leader's power by a massive injection of Twin Odin's sperm. The last two leaders had died trying to get the statue's cock into their ass. They bled to death."

"We were twins with long thin cocks. We were to be Twin Odin's stand in. Othacar told us all of this. Linked gold rings were the symbol of the god. Othacar's had selected us because he thought he could take both of our cocks. We could fuck him without being ripping him to pieces. We were popular among his men, and the combination of us being twins, having gold rings in our cocks and being able to double fuck the chieftain, might be enough to save his hide. If it didn't work, he would be killed, and we would be sacrificed on his funeral pyre."

"I bet you found yourselves longing for the Goth's ass?" interjected Otter. He guessed he could have survived the stone cocks of the statue. Everyone laughed.

"But we needed to practice to make sure Othacar could take our cocks and we could stay erect long enough to screw him. There was the problem. Othacar's cock was huge, but his hole was tight and inflexible," said Theodosius.

"How inconvenient," Maximus said. "You would think the gods would have given Othacar an ass suitable for fucking. Since his life depended on it, that would have been the least the pagan devils could do."

"He was related to the two previous chieftains, so apparently the combination of huge cock and small ass was a family tradition." Theodosius added. Unexpectedly Marcus, who had been silent since the rescue, spoke, "Othacar's father and uncle didn't have Theo and me to help them out." Hadrian wondered if perhaps Theo and Marcus had not been entirely virginal when the pirates abducted them. There seems to have been a genuine enthusiasm for the task on the part of the twins.

"And help we did. We figured if Othacar was to be fucked by the gods, he had better look as if he enjoyed it. The first time Marcus fucked him he looked as if someone had tried to shove Cleopatra's needle up his ass. He was in real pain. We only had a month to train him, between full moons and it would be a challenge," Theo explained.

"Not only was he real tight, but the magic nut was deep inside, hard to reach." Mark seems to be warming to the explanation. "But Christ was with us. I had been fucking him like a dog, without much success, but when we rolled him on is back the gold ring rammed his ass nut head on. His cock extended to its full size and he understood what we were trying to do. He was a strong man, and once he realized the feeling he was after, he could deal with any amount of pain, to feel my cock head and the ring again."

Theo added, "We had a second problem, Othacar was a big man. He had a big cock, big ass, and big gut. The two of us fucked him one after the other for hours and as we wore a groove in his butt. He responded better and better, but how would we physically get both our cocks in his ass. The hairy ass and hairy gut made this almost impossible.

"Othacar would add a third ring to unite our cocks for the "blessed Union" Mark was to lie down, Othacar was to squat on it, he was to roll back and envelop them and fill his ass. We were young, thin, and flexible. We figured his weight might break a bone or two, but at least our cocks would safely lodge in his ass. A broken bone is preferable to the funeral pyre. We tried it and it worked well enough."

"On the day of the divine fucking we were nervous as hell, so was Othacar. We had spent so much time in his ass he was almost a third brother. The wise man came in and chanted some mumbo jumbo. We silently said the Our Father. He gave us something to drink, told us to bend over and shoved something in our asses. It turned out later it was a carved stone that had a bump in a place that pushed the prostate. Athgar came in clamped on the third ring uniting our two cocks and began sucking both of us."

"As he sucked our cocks the stone in our asses seemed to warm up and we were suddenly more excited we had ever been before. We went into the room, filled with Othacar's warriors, all dressed. We were naked with full erections. Othacar roared and entered the room, naked with an erection that impressed everyone in to room. He came over to us and grabbed us, kissed us and carried both of us to the platform. We were cock-to-cock, erection to erection, he straddled us, positioned his ass above the middle ring and took us both. He was hot! He sat back and squirmed to get deeper penetration, raised up again, rotated quarter turn and sat down again. He did this four times, facing north, south, east and west, and making sure everyone in the room got a full view of the three rings and two cocks entering his ass."

Othacar was producing enough pre-cum to lube every ass in the room. His cock was rock hard and glistening in the torch light and he settled in for a good ass grinding fuck. Othacar returned to the east position, that must have had both cocks and three rings ramming his prostate, and he just bellowed. Athgar came up to me and the wise man went to Marc and fed us their cocks. Othacar's ass was always tight, and the feel of my brother's cock rubbing against my cock deep in the chieftain's ass pushed me over the edge. We always shoot together, so we filled Othacar with our semen. We normally convulse when each spurt shoots, so we amplified this, screaming, "Othacar, you are the chosen one!"

Everyone in the room had a raging hard on by this time and was laughing. Fox was sucking Marcus, and Optimus was still caressing Theo's cock. "Did they fall for it?" asked Bembo.

"They sure did!" said Marcus. "Whether it was our fucking abilities, our acting abilities, or my lucky discovery of Othacar's prostate, I don't know. By the way, the wise man had slipped some of the potion he gave to us into the mead served to the warrior troop. They were all erect."

Theo added, "Othacar was a man possessed, and prowled the room for the rest of the might, looking for fuck mates. I don't know how many men he screwed that night, but had they been women, he would have doubled the population of the tribe."

Everyone got drunk and eventually passed out. Athgar removed the third ring, and we fell asleep in each other's arms.

"What happened then?" Hadrian asked.

"That's a story for another night," Marc said. "You know we were chained up a week on ship, without any way to even touch our cocks. I was hoping you men might be able to lighten out load." Everyone was willing to help.

CHAPTER FOUR

Two Bears and a Boy

Optimus and Julian were on watch that night. "I have never done anything like that," confessed the magistrate. "I am uncomfortable with what happened earlier tonight."

"I have never felt anything like your cock!" Julian said. "I hope we can spend many happy hours finding ways to get your cock and my ass to get better acquainted."

"I couldn't believe I could do that in front of all the men. For years I spent hours trying to find ways of hiding my relationship with Maximus. All of a sudden I am fucking a stranger in the middle of a group of strangers." Optimus continued.

"No man is a stranger once you have fucked him. Believe me, we are friends now!" chuckled Julian. "I didn't know a patrician magistrate could be so well hung. I bet you never guessed how hot a blacksmith's ass could be?"

"You're right there. Wolf's cock was the real shock. I had never tasted anything like that before. My tongue was inside his skin and his skin inside my mouth. I was trying to drive this hairy animal crazy with my tongue licking his cock head." Optimus sighed with longing. "It was hard to believe my tongue could do to such a big man. Once he shot his load in my mouth, I was so excited I had to fill something with my sperm."

"Well, I am glad I was there." Julian joked, but there was a suggestion of sincerity in his voice. "I had guessed Wolf had considerable recreational potential. He always held back with the Boys and me. We've been together, slept together, and all our sexual relationships have been in full view. We seem to be just as close as we ever have been. I think men have different standards when their cocks do their thinking. We all know what is going on, we all understand. There may be people who have never had a cock in their ass and their cocks have never spewed in a spectacular climax, but for those who have experienced it, they know what a man is feeling and what it takes to get him there."

"Wolf liked it as much as I did?" Optimus asked.

"And I liked it as much as you did," Julian added. "There wasn't a man in the room that would not have liked to have been where you were. And most men would have loved to have been where I was with you pumping the shit out of me and fucking me to the top of Mount Olympus." Julian then dropped to his knees, opened Optimus' robe and took the cock. This time he had no problem deep throating the whole thing.

The next morning when the sun rose, the entire group seemed to be more at ease. The Britons continued to defer to the Roman Patricians, but their greetings were warmer than they had been before. They all felt they were all in this place together, and all could work together. After several weeks, they decided to search the countryside for additional items necessary for survival. The entire district was depopulated and abandoned. However, Hadrian remembered the area as being rich, with productive fields and orchards. He also recalled streams filled with plentiful fish and woods filled with game. They decided to send several teams out into the countryside.

Optimus, Fox and Badger made up the first team who searched to the west along the coast. By noon they came upon the ruins of a large seaside villa. Here the destruction was far more complete than had been visible in the other villas in the area. Optimus, who had traveled extensively, at first thought it looked as if an earthquake had hit the villa followed by a fire. A concerted effort had been made to overturn walls and columns. Where frescoes and mosaics remained, someone had scraped out the faces.

It had been a large and almost palatial villa. To the rear in the service quarters Fox found a long building with two broad benches on each long wall. Embedded iron shackles in the walls and floors meant this had been the slave quarters. The master of the house shackled the slaves as if they were criminals and working in the mines or on the galleys. You never used shackles for farm hands. Optimus wondered if the cruel treatment might have caused of the slave insurrection that devastated the district.

The slaves stripped the villa of anything of value, and smashed anything they couldn't carry. Optimus knew the slaves would not have carried off the most important items there, the seeds and roots could help him to re-establish a garden. He quickly located the former gardens. They had been vast, but now were weed clogged. Many plants reverted to their wild state, but Optimus was confident he could find enough for his purposes.

As he searched through the remains, Badger came up to him and whispered, "Get Fox and follow me, there is something you need to see."

Optimus waved to Fox and the men followed Badger across the field, and into a forested area. The under growth was thick, and almost impassible, but Badger had found a path though the thorns. A few hundred paces inside the woods a crude hut sat in a clearing. A small fire with a weak stream of smoke drifted into the sky from inside the hut. Two big bear like men and younger man were outside. The older men were almost identical in size and physique. Both were of middle height, very muscular and bearded. One was dark skinned and covered in pitch-black hair; brilliant copper colored hair covered the other light-skinned man. The youth was slight, almost emaciated and pale.

All three were naked. The boy fucked the red bear who was on his back on the ground as the dark bear fed his cock to the boy. The boy was deep dicking the red bearded man pulling his long and meaty cock all the way out so the head alone remained in the ass, then shoving it in. The cock was the only non-emaciated element on the youth's body. Fox moved forward, but Optimus stopped him and whispered, "Let them finish, they look close."

The two bears moaned in pleasure. The youth pulled his cock out and shot a bucketful of cum onto the red bear's chest. The young man stopped sucking the black bear's cock. The three observers watched as the black bear ejaculated. His seed arched over the boy's shoulders and landed on the ground. The sun caught the sperm on its flight. It was brilliant white ribbon of sperm against the gloomy darkness of the woods. Optimus thought it looked like one of the trick fountains he had seen in Rome years before.

The black bear bellowed, "God that was good!" He spoke Latin with a pronounced Greek accent. "I can't remember the last time I emptied my balls!"

"Stick it back in again, get me off, Paulus!" the red bear begged. His Latin had a British twang.

"I don't know if it is still hard enough," the young man said in schoolhouse Latin. He shoved it in the open ass. The red bear shuddered as his cock erupted. It indeed erupted. Seed emerged as a lava flow, gushing from the cock as the man's entire body twitched uncontrollably. It was a sexual earthquake.

"Greetings Romans!" Optimus announced his presence. The boy started and lost his erection. His cock slipped out of the red haired man's ass. The red bear was still twitching and apparently didn't notice the stranger's voice. The black bear seemed unconcerned, and looked at the new comers.

"Greeting Romans!" the black haired bear said. That he was naked, half erect, and defenseless did not affect him. "How is it you are here?" he asked.

"Escaping from the Saxon onslaught," answered Optimus. "I am Optimus, former magistrate from Verulamium, and these are my associates, Badger and Fox."

"I am Orsinian, the Armenian Bear, and my associate is Cedric, the British Bruin," replied the black bear with a formal and rather theatrical flourish.

Both Fox and Badger said together. "Wrestlers!" Optimus had no idea what they meant.

"Actually, former wrestlers," said the man who was Cedric. He had risen to his feet and entered the conversation, not worried there still was cum dripping from his half-erect cock. "We gave that up several years ago, I am a carpenter, and Orsinian is a stone mason. We too are trying to avoid the Saxon visitors. By the way, are they near?" his casual intonations did not disguise the genuine concern in his voice.

"We have seen none," replied Optimus, "none alive. We think they are to the east of us a good distance." Fox and Badger were looking at the two wrestlers with frank admiration. They were impressive specimens, even if they looked a bit the worse for wear. "And who is your young companion?" Optimus asked.

"I am Paulus, son of Agrippa, Count of the Saxon Shore," the boy answered, obviously trying to achieve the self-assurance of the two wrestlers. Optimus felt a lump in his stomach. Barbarians over ran the Saxon shore fortresses two years earlier. The Count and most of his men died defending them. Optimus was surprised the boy had survived.

"We seem to be in identical circumstances," observed Orsinian. "Brothers in flight. Welcome to our humble abode." Years of performances before the public seemed to have permanently affected the man's speech. "Paulus, get some food for our guests."

Fox said he had seen the men wrestle years earlier, and Optimus gathered they were celebrities. Cedric told their stories. "We retired five years ago, and decided to settle in Londinium, where there is still a call for men with our skills. There was no new construction, but many buildings needed repairs. We know the methods of fine construction. We were working on a villa to the south of Londinium when the Saxon advanced and cut us off from home. We decided south and west were the direction to go, but we weren't familiar with the country. I am afraid we were true sons of Rome, frankly scavenging for food in the countryside has been difficult. This last month has been hell."

Fox then told them the story of their flight and arrival at the seaside villa. Optimus thought these men would be a good addition to the group, but he realized Fox was actively trying to recruit them. Wrestlers often fought nude and clearly Orsinian and Cedric didn't mind being nude. They were fully aware of the appeal of their bodies, and of their cocks. The boy was trying to emulate them, without much success, although his donkey dong was even more impressive than the thick wrestler meat. Optimus asked Paulus to tell his story.

"I was at a school in Londinium when the barbarians captured the fortress and killed my father. He wanted me to be an educated man. When the teacher realized my father was dead, most probably with my mother and sisters, he turned me out on the street, taking all of my clothes for "unpaid bills." For a while, I worked for food in an inn, but I decided to try to find out if anyone survived, and left for the Saxon shore. It was a foolish idea, I have been lost for a year, and just ran into Cedric and Orsinian at the last full moon," explained Paulus.

Optimus felt some sympathy. Rome had been an urban empire; many of the citizens were accustomed to the qualities of the city, the baths, theaters and markets. They knew nothing of growing vegetables, fishing or hunting. Without Roman mileposts and roads, they were lost in the countryside. "How old are you boy?" Optimus asked.

"I am a man, and wore the toga," he replied. "I think I am eighteen or nineteen. It has been hard to keep the years straight."

Badger thought the boy looked younger, but several years of poor food might make him look younger. There was no question; however, his cock was fully adult. He sported a beard.

Orsinian added, "Paulus was good enough to take us into his home. He may be young, but he is a gentleman."

"Whatever he shoved in my ass was adult! I can vouch for that!" Cedric said. "Pure man cock!"

Everyone laughed, and Optimus even forgot to be shocked at the frankness of the two wrestlers. "Your performance was exciting," Optimus said.

"Did you go to matches?" Cedric asked Optimus. It was clear Fox and Badger did.

"I never did," confessed the magistrate.

"Real wrestlers fight nude, really close with lots contact between the wrestlers and their opponent's equipment. Usually the winner screws the loser. You are so excited by the end of a match you need to drop a load somewhere." Orsinian explained. "In the old days the victory fuck took place out of sight. I guess in an olive grove or wherever else those Greeks might find conducive to passion. But for us professional wrestlers, we found out some men and women in the audience would pay more to watch the fuck than the match."

"Orsinian is a good wrestler, but a great fucker," Cedric added. "He once had one of those strange eastern queens come and watch. She got so excited, she stripped during the performance and she had him pull out of my ass just as he was ready to shoot, and she opened wide and took the load in her cunt. For good measure, I shot my own load in there. If you ever hear of an eastern potentate who had twins, one with red hair and one with black, that was us!"

Everyone laughed. "Did Paulus defeat you?" Badger asked.

"Hell no! It was pure fun!" answered Cedric. "Fun and curiosity, I had never been fucked by a cock that big, never been fucked by a virgin! Paulus deserved to learn from a friend." Cedric walked over and tousled the boy's hair. Paulus blushed but his cock began to rise.

Optimus suggested they all go back to the subterranean villa and look it over. All six of the men realized the bears and Paulus wouldn't return to the clearing in the woods. Optimus thought they would be both helpful, useful, and they clearly would be congenial. When Orsinian and Cedric emerged from the hut with the tools they had kept with then, and a varied collection of weapons we knew they would be helpful. Like Bembo, hauling heavy weights was no problem to the men. Paulus turned out to be the perfect scout. He moved making no noise, effortlessly vanishing into the landscape.

They returned to the villa, and the new comers were accepted with enthusiasm. The two bears looked at the ruined villa with a professional air and seemed to have a clear view of what they needed to do. The subterranean villa impressed them. Orsinian looked puzzled. He disappeared, and a short time later, the men standing in the thermal pool room saw light coming from a skylight. Orsinian had found an alabaster covered skylight and uncovered it. Leaves and debris covered the feature.

For an accidental assemblage of men, the group had a good distribution of the skills necessary to survive in a burned out villa in a land overrun by barbarians. The Britons were good hunters and fishermen. Optimus had managed estates and farmed. Julian could both repair and create useful items as well as weapons. Hadrian was could manage household planning. Finding the food, clothes and other elements needed to keep life going was his skill. It was early summer, but he knew winter was coming, and he would be ready. Bembo was a beast of burden, and cleaning man. The bears could both build and fight. Maximus thought, planned and schemed. Originally, every one shared tasks such as cooking, but some men clearly had skills lacking in others. Maximus could cook, and liked to cook. Optimus soon took charge of the abandoned fields and found enough surviving plants to re-establish a garden.

The twins and Bembo were familiar with baths, and soon had the sanitation and bathing facilities working as well as any in the land. With Cedric and Orsinian's skills, the building began to look as it had before the fire. They were careful to insure the scene of desolation remained on the outside of the building. All the repairs were on the interior, camouflaged from view.

As the sun set on the night of their arrival, Orsinian and Cedric put on their special wrestling performance. It was athletic, comic and ribald. They ended with the story of the eastern queen and asked for a volunteer to play the queen. Much to everyone's surprise, before Otter could offer his ass, Optimus stood up and stepped forward. He gave a mime of the queen in heat stripping naked and dancing around the two wrestlers as they coupled. He then skewered himself on Orsinian's cock just as it vacated Cedric's ass. Orsinian pumped his load into the magistrate's ass and then turned and invited Cedric to do the same. The men were rolling on the floor when Optimus did a pantomime of the queen trying to give birth to twins through his horse dick. Everyone slept well that night.

Optimus woke to find someone next to him. It was Paulus. Optimus felt the boy's erect cock, played with it until pre-cum covered it; he then opened his legs and drew them up so the boy's cock would get in. Paulus toyed with Optimus' hole for a while, just inserting his cock head it. Then he plunged in.

It was a strange sensation for Optimus, the boy's cock was so long, and he wondered when it would fill him. Soon he was stretched to the limit and enjoying every minute of the experience. Paulus was slow and took his time, silently climaxing deep in the ass. When he pulled out Optimus asked, "Was it my ass you were after, or was it the feel of Orsinian's and Cedric's cum on your cock you wanted?"

"It started as their seed," Paulus answered, "but it ended up being your ass." The two men then fell asleep.

The next morning Maximus stated he was going to put some meat on Paulus emaciated frame. Within two months, the combination of Maximus' attention, and the exercise he got from helping the bears repair the villa transformed the boy. He was indeed a man. Orsinian eventually found three more skylights and several ventilation tunnels. The roof lights in the warm pool apparently were forgotten long before the fire. Torches illuminated the room, covering the entire space in black soot.

The twins and Paulus started to clean the walls and they found fine marbles covering the lower part of the walls. Above that band, complexly frescoed images of gods covered the domed ceiling. They were in the style of ancient Greek paintings with nude black figured men against a terra cotta background.

In the lowest tier, the gods were dancing with their arms intertwined, each with the modest penises were typical of Greek painting. In the second tier they were embracing, and were sporting erections. On the third tier they were fucking, cock in ass, forming a continuous ring. Jupiter was fucking Hercules who was fucking Neptune. Neptune had his big, shell shaped cock in Apollo's tender ass. At the end of the ring, Priapus, the cock-god had his monster dong in Jupiter's hole. Hadrian looked up at the cleaned room, he and knew what the room had been used for. He hoped to use it again for the same purpose.

Most of the men were sitting around the pool during a torrential downpour, when they noticed water showering from the ceiling. They first thought it was a leak, but then realized the water was coming from the erect cocks of the second tier. The cocks connected to a rain gutter. As the men frolicked under the shower, Maximus thought - oh the glories that were Rome!

CHAPTER FIVE

A Third Bear Appears

A few days later after the arrival of the two bears and the boy, Hadrian and Bembo set off to the east looking for the orchards Hadrian remembered so well. They were a half day away when they saw birds circling above, and they had the uncomfortable feeling death was near. They confirmed their suspicions as the stench grew and became more pronounced. They moved slowly until they were next to a scene of desolation. The summer was hot; decomposition set in quickly. There seemed to be bodies everywhere, perhaps twenty of them.

Most were Saxons, but in the middle of the piles of bodies and severed limbs were Britons. There was no sign of life and the two men came closer. Clearly, the Britons had inflicted tremendous casualties on the Saxons as they fought the good fight. They clearly had not triumphed. Every collection of barbarians had a Briton at its core.

Hadrian realized possibly no one had been victorious, since the clothes and jewelry on the bodies was intact; no one had striped the bodies of their valuables. There was a moan, and the two men froze. Bembo quickly took one of the swords from the bodies, and stood at alert. There was a second moan.

They moved in the direction of the sound and looked at the biggest pile of bodies. Six dead Saxons made a ring around a richly dressed Briton. Bembo touched one of the Germans. He was stone cold. He then tried each of the others with the same result. All were dead. He then touched the Briton. "He's alive," he said. Hadrian looked closely.

"The man is of high rank," he observed, "and he is a big man." The man must have been as big as Bembo, but was as blond as Bembo was dark, and as hairy as Bembo was hairless. The man had a mane of hair and beard and mustache. His body was as hairy as his head. You could see it through his ripped clothes.

Blood and gore from his many wounds covered him. Yet his heart was still beating. "What should we do with him?" asked Bembo.

"Let's take him home," Hadrian suggested. "He is a big man. He could be useful."

"How can we get him back?" asked Bembo.

Hadrian realized all of the clothes, robes and cloaks of the dead were available for use. With the trunks of some saplings, they could make a stretcher. Bembo and Hadrian were both attracted to the all but dead man and were willing to try to save him. Bembo found some suitable trees, and Hadrian tried to bind up the worst of the wounds. The man had suffered a major blow to his head, a gash in his leg and had a broken arm. Hadrian figured the leg was broken also.

One of the cloaks of the dead men and the jeweled broaches of the others made it possible to make a stretcher. When they lifted him on to it, he screamed, but he must have passed out from the pain, and they were able to carry him.

It was well after dark when they returned to the villa. Bembo had no problem with the weight of the man; Hadrian was all but dead. The body caused a stir, and remarkably was still alive. Optimus had been trained as a doctor, and quickly set to work.

Hadrian had hoped to get credit for his find, but sat down and fell asleep, and didn't wake up until the next day. He awoke in the domed central chamber of the underground villa, with a great blond body next to him, naked and still. "Oh shit, he died!" he thought, but he decided to feel the body to make sure. When he reached over, the worst pain he had ever felt almost overcame him. It was as if every cramp and everybody ache he had ever felt was concentrated in his arms and shoulders. The pain was so bad he was winded. He cried out and Bembo's head popped up.

"I don't think you are accustomed to carrying men for long distances," Bembo sounded serious, but his eyes were laughing.

"I think not. Is he alive?" asked Hadrian.

"Yes, we cleaned him up. The magistrate says we need to set his leg and arm sometime today, or he will be a cripple. Magister Optimus also thinks something may be broken inside him." Bembo replied. Hadrian was going to comment, but was so exhausted he decided not to. The pain subsided and he fell asleep again.

He woke up to the Briton's screams. Optimus and Julian were setting his leg and arm. Broken bodies were all part of a smith's business, and Julian was knowledgeable and helpful. The man again passed out from the pain, and all was quiet again. Hadrian got up, and while it seemed as if every muscle in his body ached, at least he was able to move. He went outside.

Maximus had recognized the body. The man was Arcturus Ambrosianus, a Romanized Briton and a member of a distinguished family. He must have been heading east to fight the Saxons when his group of noblemen fell into a Saxon scouting party. Arcturus and his men must have fought bravely and effectively. They were too badly outnumbered.

He spoke to Arcturus during one of his few lucid moments. The man remembered only the battle and nothing else. Months later Arcturus described the weeks of pain to Maximus. He couldn't think; he couldn't orient himself. He wasn't sure if Saxons captured him, or if his men rescued him. When he realized the men around him were Latin speaking, he relaxed, but the pain was constant. The pain was constant until he moved, when it became unbearable.

Everything would vanish into oblivion and then he would wake again. The pain would return. He recalled being carried, and then lowered into warm water. The water was wonderful, but then he was taken out and returned to a dark room. He tried to sit up, and was again overwhelmed by pain.

He had nightmares, of fighting the Saxons, of trying to please his father, of chasing wild animals. There were other dreams. He felt his cock touched by soft wet things that licked it. At first soft and delicate, but later he thought something was after is balls, trying to suck them out of his body, through his cock.

He felt other things, sexual. He felt sexual excitement coming from inside his body. He had screwed women and knew about the stimulation of his cock, but this feeling came from inside. Arcturus couldn't think straight, the nightmares, the pain and the dreams all melded together.

The British noble was a handsome and wealthy man, about twenty-five. He was unaware of the stir he had caused in this isolated group of men. There was no shortage of men willing to nurse him back to health.

Hadrian and Bembo took turns watching over the man. They found him; they felt ownership of him. Arcturus' bad dreams were the product of his recent experiences and his subconscious. Hadrian produced his sexual fantasies.

Hadrian had been the chief butler for the patrician household of Ceralis Patellius. One of his duties was to serve as nurse to the men of the household. He was genuinely helpful, and had considerable knowledge of medicinal herbs and spices. Sitting beside the sick bed, Hadrian had found a little sex play could help while away the hours, for both him and the patient. He told his mistress he had a magic sleeping potion, but it would only work for men.

Hadrian started by massaging the sore muscles of the patient. It was more a rubbing and caressing than a massage, but it seemed to relax. He then moved slowly closer to the genitals, massaging them with a feather like touch. Ceralis himself admitted that when he was recovering from a serious head injury, it was days before he figured out what Hadrian was doing. Ceralis knew Hadrian sexual skills first hand.

The tongue was the most delicate instrument in Hadrian' toolbox, and he would touch and caress the cock, never actually sucking it. Eventually the patient would be erect, and Hadrian would change his attention from the relatively insensitive foreskin to the much more responsive cock head. Ceralis' twenty-year-old cousin and his eighteen-year-old son were the only patients who actually climaxed at this point. Hadrian had a theory old, stale sperm, cooped up in the balls was bad for you. You needed to expel it and make new. He had actually tried to explain this to a doctor once, who told him he was crazy.

Hadrian knew once the sperm started to flow again, the patient was well on the road to recovery. It had worked many times. Hadrian's objective was to make the patient climax without the stress and excitement of conscious sexual contact. If the tongue bath on the cock head didn't work, Hadrian continued to stimulate the head, while he worked a finger into the ass. This was a very slow process, but eventually he would touch the prostate. Usually the patient was unaware; at most he felt a mild fullness in his ass, and the warmth of the stimulated gland. The finger didn't have the sledgehammer like effect a hard penis did, but it worked.

No one ever awoke during this process. Hadrian was well aware he could not have been that delicate, and was convinced several of those in his care were just enjoying themselves. That was all to the better.

Arcturus was difficult for Hadrian. He was much more badly hurt than most of those who had been in his care, and he was far more attractive. Hadrian was very active sexually and sometimes tended to have a workman-like, rather than passionate interest in most men. Hadrian did not have a workman-like interest in Arcturus. He was immensely attracted to the blond, hairy giant. Years before Julian and he had joked about finding the Cock of the Gods. Arcturus had the penis that would have made Jupiter crazed with lust. Priapus would drool in envy. Hadrian was convinced he had found that cock, lying between the legs of the British giant.

He wasn't sure for the man was unconscious most of the time, and there was no trace of an erection, but it was big. The balls were the size of apples, contained in a wrinkled, hair covered sack. Relaxed, the cock was the length of a man's hand, and encased in a thick skin sheath that hung loosely. It looked like it could be stretched to hold an incredible fuck tool.

On one hand, Hadrian was afraid the man might die before he had a chance to taste it, to savor it. On the other hand, Arcturus was in such poor condition, it might not be possible to get near it without hurting him. In the back of his mind, Hadrian feared the man might not appreciate the treatment; he might not respond.

Hadrian was always a considerate nurse, and the first night he simply tended to the needs of the man, and pondered the problem. By dawn, he made a decision. If the man died, he died, and it didn't make any difference if he had balls filled with cum or not. The seed drained from his balls wouldn't affect the giant's ascent to heaven.

The technical problems of getting to the cock were more difficult. Fortunately, there was Bembo. Hadrian explained his medical theory to Bembo, and it struck the former furnace man as both sensible and compassionate. He recalled the many times Fulvius had felt both relaxed and reinvigorated after shooting a load. Fulvius had said many times he wanted to die with a smile on his face and his chest covered in sperm.

Bembo volunteered to support Hadrian in this delicate operation, holding him just above the Briton's cock, so Hadrian could get access without applying pressure to the man's battered body. The next night they got Arcturus to eat a thick broth made by Maximus to help build up strength, and then lowered him slowly into the warm pool, both cleaning him and relaxing him. The put him back on the bed to sleep. He had a fever and they didn't cover him to prevent him from getting too hot.

After he fell into a deep but restless sleep, Hadrian leaned over and licked the puckered opening of Arcturus' foreskin. Hadrian was no stranger to lust, but he was shaking like a leaf. Bembo supported him by grabbing his tunic and essentially hanging him above the cock.

After a short while, the trembling stopped and Hadrian began a slow and thorough exploration of the Briton's cock. Bembo just held him there, noticing Hadrian seemed to show the same tenderness, almost worship Fulvius had once lavished on Bembo's cock.

Excited anticipation can create unrealistic expectations, and Hadrian' expectations of Arcturus was well beyond reasonableness. Hadrian could not believe the increased attraction he felt once he made physical contact with the cock. He licked the puckered opening several dozen times and the opening began to part. He slowly worked his tongue into the hole, and began slow circular movements with his tongue opening and spreading the skin. He felt a deep urge to swallow the entire thing, but he resisted. It was excruciating and unbelievably exciting. "Pull me up Bembo, I can't take it anymore." Hadrian whispered.

The both walked over to the pool, stripped, and sank into the warm water. "I think he was responding," said Bembo, "It was rising some; the cock head was moving down the tube."

"I think so too, but I'm not sure I can do it, I have never been so excited in my life," agreed Hadrian. Both men had full erections. "There are cocks and there are cocks, but he has something remarkable. Do you think he knows?"

"Fulvius was an ugly dirty old man, and he told me he loved me a thousand times. I never believed him until he made love to my cock. My cock told me he really cared for me. The first time my cock touched his prostate I knew it was real. I never felt anything for him, just gratitude, but he actually loved me. I wish now my cock had shot its load deep into his brain, and told him I loved him, but I didn't and it didn't. Cocks don't lie," Bembo mused.

"Well we'd better get back to work," said Hadrian. They returned to the sleeping body, and Hadrian hovered above the cock like a hummingbird at a pollen-filled flower. By the end of the night, the tip of the cock head had emerged, and while Arcturus' cock was by no means erect, Hadrian could appreciate its true scale.

Bembo pulled Hadrian up, and they looked at the calm, sleeping man. "Look!" Bembo whispered. Emerging from the half-enshrouded cock head was a single glistening bead of liquid. He lowered Hadrian down again and so he could collect it on his tongue. Bembo pulled him up again; the two men faced each other and kissed, sharing the drop.

After they broke apart, Hadrian spit on his hand and lubricated Bembo's erect cock. Hadrian bent over and Bembo shoved his cock deep into Hadrian ass. Bembo used one arm to pin Hadrian hairy chest, the other hand grabbed the ridged cock. Bembo quickly pumped three or four times and Hadrian shot cum all over his hairy gut and chest. Bembo rubbed it in, spreading it evenly over the nude torso. A few thrusts later Bembo filled Hadrian' ass. The two men collapsed on the floor.

"That wasn't love," Bembo murmured.

"Shit no! I've never needed a fucking so bad in my life," said Hadrian. "Thank you." Later, Hadrian looked back and realized even though Bembo covered him in cum, and filled his ass with it, the taste of Arcturus' one bead of pre-cum remained in his mind.

The next night Hadrian coaxed the entire head out of the enveloping foreskin, and introduced a finger in the ass. The British nobleman responded with a much larger offering of pre-cum, and some movements Hadrian interpreted and trying to get a more comfortable hold on the new object in his ass.

When Arcturus was conscious, Hadrian persistence got quite a bit of food in him, bathed him in the thermal pool and cleaned his wounds of anything that looked like puss or infection. Movement was an ordeal for the man, but Julian was convinced unless he moved he would stiffen up like a board and die.

On the third night, Hadrian's finger made contact with Arcturus' prostate. The cock had been half-erect, and the entire head exposed when Hadrian two fingers touched the gland. Hadrian remembered when he first touched another man's magic nut. It had been Julian's and Julian had been resisting Hadrian's advancing finger when the finger and the nut made contact and Julian suddenly relaxed and opened his ass as wide as he could. It was soft and squishy and the size of a hazelnut or acorn. After Hadrian massaged it and gave it a few good pokes, Julian was crying, desperately needing release.

Arcturus' was the size of a ripe plum, in a good year. If Arcturus has been conscious, and willing, Hadrian would have caressed it with three fingers and held the whole thing in his hands. With one finger on each side of it, Hadrian began slowly massaging it. Slowly and delicately he kneaded the gland, and watched the cock grow to full erection. By then the pre-cum was dripping from the head, down the shaft and into the reddish blond bush. Bembo was supporting Hadrian so he did not apply any pressure to the body while he manipulated it, and felt the increase in sexual tension as he watched the cock get bigger and Hadrian pick up the pace of the prostate massage.

Hadrian was exhausted, and ready to give up for the night, when Bembo's cock touched Hadrian' asshole and the mushroom head slipped just inside the sphincter. Hadrian involuntarily jabbed his fingers forward, and poked Arcturus' prostate. Immediately the gland began to fill up, and became hard as a rock. Sperm shot high in the sky covering Hadrian and Arcturus with long ribbons of cum, landing on the hairy bodies of the two men.

Bembo pulled Hadrian up, and firmly skewered him on his cock, Hadrian shot and all of Hadrian's cum landed on Arcturus. There the sperm merged. Bembo spent much of his life cleaning up the public baths, so he deposited his load deep inside Hadrian. He didn't like mess. Bembo kept his cock deep in the ass for a while, giving a little pump once and a while to work the last bit of sperm out of the cock. Hadrian used his finger to collect the ribbons of semen, which draped Arcturus' body, and then sucked the man juice off the finger. Hadrian was convinced the man who possessed the cock of the gods had turned the corner, and would live.

As the sun rose and Optimus came in to relieve the two men of their nursing duties. Hadrian told him this theory. Optimus laughed and told him to get some sleep. Optimus had considerable medical knowledge, and knew the butler's medical theories were comic. However, Arcturus showed considerable improvement when he woke. He was actually hungry and wanted to eat. He even walked a few paces using Wolf and Fox as crutches.

A week later Arcturus was a vigorous, energetic man, moving with either Fox or Wolf as a crutch and with his arm in a sling. It was clear he was a leader of men, physically appealing, intelligent, and possessing a knack for getting along with other men. Hadrian continued his evening treatments. Now he was sure the blond man knew what was going on.

Hadrian also noticed more often than not Arcturus had his arm around a man, or was sitting, touching his neighbor. Even Wolf and Optimus, the most reserved men in the group didn't seem to mind it. Arcturus seemed to like men, and liked physical contact with men. Did he like to fuck men? Did he like to play with men?

CHAPTER SIX

New Discoveries

Arcturus was eager to become a functioning member of the group and volunteered to stand watch. Optimus thought he needed to rest and complete his recovery, but Arcturus insisted, pointing out you didn't need to use two arms to stand watch. His first watch was with Paulus. Paulus had filled out in the intervening weeks since he arrived at the villa and was turning into a lean, muscular and handsome man. The dichotomy between his thin body and huge cock was being resolved.

Arcturus knew much about Agrippa, Paulus' father. He had been a Romanized nobleman of the Atribate tribe. When the emperor withdrew the legions from Britain to fight the Goths in Gaul, Agrippa was one of those who stepped in to fill the void. A man of ability, he rose to become the Count of the Saxon Shore, the man in charge of the coastal defenses of southern Britain.

The homegrown effort was successful for many years, but when the major onslaught came, it proved to be inadequate. Many of the local volunteers fled or deserted their posts. The barbarians killed the men who remained along with their families who lived in the coastal fortresses with the soldiers.

"I can barely remember my father," Paulus said. "He was always away, inspecting something or trying to repair this or that. Duty was everything for him, and there never were enough men to do the work needed. When he died, I lost everything I might have had. A man with no family is a nothing."

"I remember my father too well," Arcturus observed. "He was a vain overbearing man, who demanded to much of those around him, and little of himself. Actually he demanded nothing of his favorites and much of those he didn't like."

"He didn't like you?" asked Paulus.

"He despised me and my mother. She was wealthy and independent. My mother was a distant relation of Bodiccia. She would have made a great warrior queen. They hated each other. I was the product of the bridal night, born nine months after the wedding. She died when I was seven, and I was just a souvenir of a bad memory," explained Arcturus. "He had several children by his secondary wife, and screwed half of the women of the clan."

"Fortunately I had friends, boys I grew up with. I went to spend time with my mother's family when I was fourteen. They hated my father as much as my mother did, but fortunately I am the image of her grandfather, the great warlord, and they didn't think I was tainted by his blood."

"When I returned to my father's house, you could curry favor by treating me badly, and many did. Fortunately my boyhood friends didn't care about him, and, at sixteen, I was a big man. I could take care of myself. My friends later told me they were worried about poison, but little else. Anyone who tried a physical assault would regret it, and quickly."

"You are lucky to have such companions," Paulus said.

"Had," replied Arcturus. "They were the men who died around me when the Saxons attacked us. All are dead. I loved those men and they are gone."

The men were silent for a while. The night had turned cold, Paulus was shivering has he scanned the dark sea from the villa's terrace. Arcturus walked up behind him and wrapped him in his cloak and the men shared their warmth.

"You are among friends here," Paulus said.

That night Hadrian waited for Arcturus to return from his watch and to fall asleep. When he was asleep, Hadrian approached. Just as his tongue touched Arcturus' cock, Hadrian felt Arcturus' hands hold his head and direct his entire cock down the butler's willing throat. The cock was still soft, but was swelling, filling up Hadrian' mouth. Hadrian was excited and a bit frightened Arcturus might become fully erect and choke him. He didn't need to worry.

Arcturus pulled out, leaving only his knob in the mouth. Hadrian felt liberated, after weeks of delicately toying with the giant's cock it was a relief to suck the whole thing. Judging from the amount of pre-cum oozing from the cock, Arcturus felt good too. Hadrian sucked and worked a finger to the ass ring, pressed it into the hole and Arcturus shot off. Hadrian took the load, and continued to suck until the cock returned to its original size.

"Thank you," Arcturus whispered. "That was great. Why are you doing this?"

Hadrian launched into his explanation of the medical theory and then added, "Did I mention I like cock?"

Arcturus laughed. "I don't know about your medical skills, but your cock skills I can vouch for! What is it you touched in my ass that feels so good? I have never felt anything like that before."

The men were lying face to face and Hadrian explained about the magic nut. It was the secret sex organ. Arcturus was cupping Hadrian' cock and balls in his huge hand, had one finger on the space between the balls and hole. "Do you want to feel mine?" Hadrian asked. Immediately there was half a finger in his hole. Hadrian' cock jumped to attention. Hadrian adjusted his position to ease the exploration. Arcturus finger was bigger than some cocks Hadrian had played with.

"How will I know when I hit it?" Arcturus asked. Just then Hadrian whole body shuddered and twitched. "There it is!" He pressed it a few more times and then massaged it slowly. "It gets hard before you shoot?" Arcturus asked. Arcturus was hard again, and was surprised at how stimulated he was as he fingered Hadrian' ass.

"God yes! But go slow, I want this to last," Hadrian responded.

Arcturus partially withdrew his finger and asked. "Does a prick feel better than a finger?"

"Usually," Hadrian was speaking from experience. "When the cock hits the right spot, there is nothing better for the man with the cock and the man with the ass. The cock lubricates itself, as you get more and more excited. It's different from sucking. Nobody minds dropping a load in another man's mouth, or jerking off together, but fucking is different. Some men love it; others aren't interested. You can force them, but it's not the same as fucking a true bottom-man, who can't get enough of your cock in his ass, and will do anything in his power to keep you hard and pumping" he paused, "Have you fucked a man?"

"No," answered Arcturus. "I watched my father fuck enough women to leave a bad taste in my mouth. He liked to screw the serving girls in front of the men. He'd strip them and have a contest to see how fast you could shoot your seed into the creature. With my wife, I did what I was supposed to do. My father selected her for her ugliness, but she was a nice woman, and I got her out of his clutches and safe with her own people before I left to fight the Saxons. "

"Speed is a nice characteristic for race horses, but not in lovers," observed Hadrian. "You liked what I've been doing to you each night?"

"Oh, yes," answered Arcturus.

"But you are real excited right now, just fingering my nut and feeling me twitch with pleasure?" asked Hadrian.

"Yes I am. Really excited," Arcturus admitted.

"That is what it's all about; trying to see how much enjoyment we can get from our bodies. This isn't like marriage. There are no contracts and property settlements, there are no dowries and there will be no children to rear. A night of sexual passion and fun is, just that, a night we aren't cold and alone," Hadrian said, his inspired speech would have continued if Arcturus' finger had not squeezed the magic nut one too many times. Hadrian shot.

The butler's view of the brotherhood of men, combined with intense anal sex amused Arcturus. He saw sex as a duty or an expression of power, not a source of pleasure, and least of all pleasure for your partner. Arcturus was surrounded by men, all strong, all attractive. For his father sex in public had been a way to humiliate and embarrass. Here there was a sense of comradeship and brotherhood. He fell asleep, confused, but excited.

The days were getting shorter and nights longer. Optimus had planted some winter vegetables could help to tide them over; the boys were very good hunters, so the worst problems of the coming season were solved. The bears had repaired the central heating system. It was another Roman marvel of ingenuity, circulating the warm water from the thermal pool under the floors.

Yet the villa held one more marvel. The central room of the subterranean villa was flanked the warm bath to the left, and the cold bath to the right. Straight ahead was a large mosaic of Bacchus drinking and screwing in a gathering of satyrs and centaurs. The twin's cleaning efforts had reached this picture, and Marcus discovered Bacchus' asshole was inset. He called the others and pressed the recess. The wall opened.

They discovered the wine cellar. Amphorae of wine filled the large, cool and dry room. All were labeled and ranged from the most rare and choice vintages from Italy, to the more humble products of the villa itself. Also in the cellar were several vats of oil for use in lamps, and others for cooking.

Fox and Otter returned that afternoon from a three day scouting expedition and brought good news. The Saxon advance had been halted and the raiders were returning to their settlements in the south. Roman survivors and their British allies fought a battle in the north and inflicted serious casualties on the invaders. All knew the raiders would return next spring, they always did, but there was breathing room, time to prepare.

Wolf had returned a week earlier with a pair of dogs that seem to have instinctively found him attractive. They clearly had been trained as watchdogs, and they immediately made themselves at home in the ruins of the villa relieved to be back in human company. Christened Hellhound and Cerberus, Wolf said a mean dog is worth ten men, and the need to keep close watch diminished.

Badger had found some pigs wandering through the woods nearby. They were semi-wild, and some apparently had mated with a wild boar, but there would be domesticated meat for weeks. Maximus had planned a feast, and the combination of the Saxon reversals and the cache of wine, turned this into a truly festive occasion. Life in the villa suddenly took a dramatic change for the better. Most of the men had been together for two months and were getting to know each other and feel more comfortable.

A fierce storm blew in. The men withdrew to the underground rooms and sealed the doors. Bembo and the dogs kept watch outside. There was food; there was wine, and flickering lamps illuminated the room. Every one relaxed as the wine took effect. The warmth of the room and full bellies contributed to the general good feeling. Drowsiness set in.

Orsinian rose and bellowed, "It's time for games!"

Badger yelled, "It's not time for another visit by the eastern Queen again." The room roared with laughter.

"I, for one, wouldn't mind another visit from the eastern queen!" Orsinian replied glancing at Optimus. "But I was thinking of more general entertainment and exercise. Tag teams!"

"Who is interested in a lesson in wrestling?" Cedric asked in his best circus barker voice. "Learn from the masters or hone your skills! I chose Badger the British ramrod, and Theodosius, you shall be out ringleader!"

"And I choose Otter, and Marcus, who, I am sure, will dance rings around our pathetic opponents!" Orsinian proclaimed. "Clear a space in the middle of the room." The men moved to the edge of the room, Optimus sat with Arcturus and Wolf, Maximus with Paulus and Julian. Hadrian and Fox sat together.

All the wrestlers stripped naked. The trios of wrestlers were grotesquely mismatched, Otter and Badger were the smallest men in the group, and the twins were slight, half the weight of Orsinian and

Cedric. "And now, to make this match a little more interesting we have a secret weapon," Cedric announced. He took a small vase and poured oil on Badger and Marcus, and rubbed them down so their bodies glistened in the flickering light. Orsinian did the same with his team. Theo and Otter enjoyed themselves making sure the oil covered them totally. Orsinian made sure Otter's ass was well oiled. Orsinian then oiled only his own cock and nipples.

Everyone except Arcturus had seen the men wrestle before, so all had some ideas of what the event would be like. The room was warm so none of the men wore more than a loincloth, except for Optimus and Hadrian who had open robes and a cloth at their waist. Most showed signs of arousal. Arcturus felt the sexual energy in the room and felt his cock begin to rise.

The match began with Orsinian wrestling Marcus. The Armenian's dark skin and thick coat of hair made him look like a black bear; the light caught only the shimmer of oil on his cock head. He was half-erect and the head had freed itself from the foreskin. Marcus shimmered, his cock hung low and the light caught the reflection of the gold ring embedded in his penis.

The minute the match got underway, it was clear this type of match had been part of Orsinian and Cedric's performance. They knew exactly how to get their partners into the most suggestive and erotic positions. When they first grappled Marcus screamed for help, and Cedric ran in and pounced on Orsinian, Otter raced in to rescue the black bear and soon the center of the room had all six men rolling on the floor. All the men had raging erections, as did everyone in the audience. Maximus, who played the referee, called a time out.

The second round was between Cedric and Otter. Cedric whispered to Otter, "Bait me. Taunt me; get me all riled up. I'll do something special for you if you do it well."

Cedric said to the audience, "Gentlemen, do not stand on formality, it's hot in here, and will be a lot hotter by the end of the night." He gave a lewd wink. "Make yourselves more comfortable, and cooler." Optimus removed his robe, and the match began. Everyone in the room was nude by the end of this round.

"Come get me big boy!" Otter yelled, the danced around the red giant, punching and jabbing. "You lumbering ox, move a little slower if you can." Cedric lunged at him, caught him, but Otter slipped out, and resumed his dance and taunts. The bears had developed many a trick to deal with the problems they encountered with his routine. Oiled men can slip out of almost any grip, but they had a special grip made for especially difficult opponents. It was Otter's turn.

Cedric lunged again, and Otter escaped. Cedric then jumped him from behind and fell to his knees. As Otter tried to wiggle up, out of his grasp, Cedric shoved his thumb into Otter's ass and got a finger on each side of the balls and penis, then grabbed as hard as he could. The forced the prostate into the root of the cock. Otter stopped dead, his eyes rolled back in his head and he let out a silent scream. He was in ecstasy, and everyone in the room knew it.

At a circus or performance Cedric would pretend this had happened by accident, and would act appropriately shocked when he "discovered" what he had done. There was no need for that here, everyone was laughing, and his teammates applauded. Cedric could also feel the intense sexual excitement emanating from Otter, and wanted to keep Otter excited. He lifted Otter up above his head, maintaining his grip on his prostate, and supporting his back with his other arm, Cedric took a victory lap around the room, Otter had arched is back and was trying to grind his ass deeper on the thumb.

Cedric then lowered Otter on his back to the floor and lifted him by his ass until his shoulders touched the floor, and then yelled, "Pinned!" Optimus had to hold Arcturus to keep him from rolling on the floor he was laughing so much. Always responsible, Optimus was afraid he might injure his arm again.

"Round three!" announced Maximus. This time it was Orsinian verses Badger and Theodosius. These men had a plan. Theo noticed Orsinian always stared at the gold ring in his cock head; he seemed transfixed by the golden ring. As the match started Theo was fully erect with pre-cum leaking from the piss slit and the ring hole. As they got in the opening position, Theo knew the black bear was thinking only about the ring. Badger jumped on Orsinian's back, but the diminutive man couldn't even get his arms around the man's chest. Badger literally slid off, causing great amusement in the spectators.

The jump knocked Theo on his back with Orsinian on top. Theo scrambled to get up. Orsinian grabbed him by the shoulders, and discovered Theo's cock with the entrancing ring, were at this mouth. It was too much; he deep throated it. The cock with its golden ring disappeared into the hairy face of the Armenian. Again there was applause. Theo's cock was deep in Orsinian's mouth, and while he was savoring the cock juice and he forgot about Badger. The plan was working. Badger stroked his cock to pump it up to full erection again and then Badger shoved his well-oiled cock into the bear's ass.

The huge cock rammed deep, in one movement. It was too much for the bear. He couldn't move, he couldn't think. Marcus yelled no fair, ran to the men and skewered Badger on his thin, ringed member.

Badger felt the hard metal ring on his prostate, and his cock expanded a little, and lodged deeper in Orsinian's ass. He wanted to pump and fill the bear ass with cum, but he couldn't move. He was trapped.

"It's a draw!" Maximus proclaimed. "It's time for an intermission!" There were cries of disappointment from the spectators, but the wrestlers obeyed. "To the baths everyone!" Maximus realized that, as far as he could tell, everyone in the room had a full load of cum boiling in their balls, and he wanted everyone to share in the climax.

Arcturus was shaking. "Are you cold?" asked Wolf.

"I've never been so excited in my life," confessed Arcturus. Wolf kissed him, and Optimus dropped to his knees and sucked the two men's cocks, first Arcturus; then Wolf; then both. "To the baths! Everyone!" demanded Maximus. The three men walked into the next room. Four lamps illuminated the room. The heavy rain outside activated a shower of cold water from the erect cocks of the ceiling frescoes. The cold water caused stream to rise and create a misty air in the room. The considerable amount of wine the men imbibed enhanced the mood. No one was drunk, but no one was sober either.

Arcturus stood under the shower then dunked himself in the water then stood erection to erection with Wolf and Optimus. They got out of the water and Wolf was on his knees sucking Arcturus' cock with frenzied passion. Optimus didn't think Wolf had sucked man meat before, but he seemed to like it. Arcturus got on the floor, and began to suck Wolf, as Wolf continued his assault his cock. As Arcturus had never sucked either, Optimus lay down next to him whispering instructions.

"Just take the skin into your mouth, work your tongue into the opening. Try to suck the skin into your mouth while working your tongue deep into the hollow. Stick the tongue in deep while sucking in the tube. That's right. Have you tasted anything salty yet? Keep going deeper." Optimus was almost as excited giving the instructions as he had doing it. Hadrian was watching the scene as Paulus sucked his cock. Hadrian caught Optimus' eye as Hadrian spread open his legs to open up his hole. Optimus first thought that Hadrian wanted him to fuck Wolf, but he shook his head, Optimus pointed at Arcturus, and Hadrian nodded. Hadrian mouthed the words, "He's ready for it."

Optimus was rock hard and dripping pre-cum. Arcturus had just tasted Wolf's pre-cum for the first time, and Optimus told him the lick the sensitive underside of Wolf's engorged cock head. Optimus' ridged cock touched Arcturus' ass crack and the blond bear raised his leg to give better access.

Theo came over and lay down beside Wolf caressing his hairy chest, and rubbing Wolf's ass with the gold ring. Wolf also opened up.

Wolf and Arcturus realized they not only were sucking cock for the first time, were tasting precum for the first time, they also were going to be fucked for the first time. They were so excited they knew it had to happen, the tinge of fear they felt added to the excitement. Wolf saw Optimus' big cock, its head bloated and dripping with lube and Wolf began to suck it with as much saliva as he could to help it hit the mark. Arcturus wanted to take the gold ring into his mouth, but he was unwilling to lose his connection with Wolf's oozing cock. Someone came by, perhaps Julian, and bathed Theo and Optimus' cocks in oil.

Arcturus and Wolf returned to their frenzied cock sucking. Arcturus saw the gold ring and hard cock poke at Wolf's virgin ass. One, two, three times. Wolf stiffened. Theo pulled it out and Julian added more oil. A second time, one, two three. The gold ring vanished. Wolf stiffened again, but as the long shaft slipped into the ass, he suddenly relaxed, and began sucking Arcturus' cock with renewed vigor.

Arcturus felt a sharp pain, Optimus was big, and his cock head made five or six assaults on the sphincter, before it opened. All at once the whole horse dick was in his ass, and Arcturus thought he was going to pass out from the waves of feeling he felt every time Optimus gave him a pump. Wolf couldn't believe the entire cock had slid into Arcturus ass as easily as it did as he watched it with his mouth filled with Arcturus' meat.

Both Wolf and Arcturus were in some pain from their first fucking, but the rock hard cocks they were sucking and the increasing flow of pre-cum they tasted, told them the other was feeling good. Optimus couldn't believe he was fucking the most beautiful man he had ever seen, and Arcturus was responding so enthusiastically. "Lick the underside of the cock head!" he reminded Arcturus.

This he did, at the same time Theo adjusted his position a bit and the cock with its golden ring rammed Wolf's prostate head on. Wolf stiffened and then twitched as his cock let loose its load and flooded Arcturus' mouth. Arcturus popped and Wolf could barely swallow fast enough to keep from choking.

Optimus stopped pumping as he felt Arcturus' rectum spasm with the ejaculation. He knew that Arcturus could not feel anything more intense at the time, so he let him relax, and finished shooting. Theo pulled out just in time to shoot Arcturus in the face.

Wolf and Arcturus pulled apart, releasing their cocks. Wolf rolled on his back; he looked drained and exhausted. Theo played with the hair on his chest. Arcturus lay back for a minute, savoring Wolf's man juice, and then realized that he was still erect and filled with desire. The night was still young.

CHAPTER SEVEN

Victory Lap

Wolf was almost asleep in the warm arms of Theo, when Fox came over, lay down on the floor and began sucking Wolf's soft cock. He slowly worked his tongue into the skin so recently vacated by Arcturus and cleaned all of the cock honey.

On the other side of the room, Hadrian was on his back with Paulus slowly fucking him. Hadrian was giving Paulus advice. "Pump slow and long. Keep it slow, but deep, go all the way in. Wait until your cock starts to take control and you speed up. Do you know when you are ready to shoot? Do you get much warning?" Hadrian asked.

"I think so," replied Paulus. "I could tell I was close with Cedric."

"When you feel that, pull out, or at least most of the way out, and cool off." Hadrian suggested. "When the urge to shoot goes away, slip back into the ass and start all over again."

"Can't I just leave it in deep and wait?" asked Paulus.

"You can try, but I always shoot when the warm asshole is enveloping my cock. I can leave my cock head in the hole and then calm down enough to go back in," Hadrian said.

"Can I try it?" Paulus asked.

"Sure, be my guest!" Hadrian felt a glow of sexual warmth. Paulus continued to pump, and soon was pumping faster and faster.

"Slow down! I think you are getting too close! It's a long night." Hadrian felt the boy pull out; Paulus stayed still for a little while, and then inserted only his cock head. Paulus waited for a while until he was more relaxed, then returned to his slow, deep dicking. Hadrian was in heaven. Paulus learned well and quickly. He worked up to a climax four times and stopped just before ejaculation. Hadrian asked him to stop three times to keep his own over stimulated cock from going over the edge.

"Oh hell! I'm shooting!" Paulus said, as he pulled out and large drop of cum oozed from his cock.

"Relax quickly! See if that stops it!" Hadrian said. Paulus did what he was told; a second large gob of semen emerged. Hadrian watched the boy relax, Paulus' shoulders dropped and Hadrian watched the tension leaving his body. There was no more semen. "Did you stop in time?

"I think so," Paulus replied. "God I was close. My cock is on fire!"

"There is nothing in my ass that can feel that isn't feeling now. It's raw," Hadrian replied.

"Do you want me to stop?" asked Paulus.

"What do you think?" Hadrian said. Paulus giggled and sank his meat in the twitching ass. The boy cum had made the cock even slipperier and the cock slid in to the hilt. Hadrian gasped. He long had dreamed of being fucked for an entire night. Paulus shared both his stamina and desire.

Cedric and Orsinian were in the pool with Marcus, Otter and Badger arguing over who had won the matches. "I don't care what you say; Badger has already fucked the shit out of me in the ring. He doesn't get a second time," Orsinian said. "I don't think it was a legal hold anyway!"

"Don't talk to me about legal holds!" whined Otter,

"I've never seen a guy like it so much before!" said Cedric as he laughed, "If you had been in our act, half of the empire west of Constantinople would have seen you trying to get more of my thumb in your ass. You're the only man I've done that to that kept his erection! I deserve a victory fuck!"

"Let's compromise. I'll fuck Otter and Marcus can fuck Cedric, and we can call it even," Badger suggested. Orsinian was still stung by Badger's huge cock, and was thinking a smaller cock might be more appealing. Otter had dreamed of Badger's meat for two years, and was more than willing to try it in his ass. Cedric was hoping to introduce his prostate to the gold ring in Marcus' cock.

"Maximus!" Cedric called. "I have a duty for you to perform. You were the referee!" Maximus came over. The hairy priest had been watching Hadrian and Paulus' coupling, and was greatly excited, but the pulled himself away and came over. By then, Otter was sitting on Badger's cock and it was clear the two men would fuck to climax. Marcus was lying down on the marble floor with his pre-cum drenched cock sticking straight up into the air. Cedric straddled Marcus and squatted on the cock, positioning the gold ring at his hole. He then lowered his ass and the ring and cock head disappeared in the red bear's ass. He had great balance and was slowly raising and lowering his ass on Marcus' erect cock.

The cock in his ass didn't affect Cedric's ability to explain the problem to Maximus. He carried on a normal conversation oblivious to the sexual stimulation. "Since Badger is already occupied and I am helping Marcus, We need a substitute cock to do the victory fucking," Cedric explained. "As referee, you need to insure the Armenian Bear understands the consequences of defeat!" Maximus and Orsinian were the two hairiest men in this group of hairy men, and they both had an attraction for men like themselves. Maximus hesitated, but Orsinian came over, embraced Maximus and cradled Maximus' heavy ball sack in his hand.

"Let me work you up," Orsinian said as he dropped to his knees and inhaled Maximus' cock in his mouth. He was going to make sure this cock was well lubricated before it took the trip into his ass.

The cock was of average length, but very thick. The second time Orsinian deep throated it; Maximus let loose a huge shot of cock juice. At first he thought Maximus had shot off, but when he swirled it around with his tongue, he realized it was pre-cum. Every second or third time he went down on it, Maximus rewarded Orsinian with another glob.

Orsinian stopped sucking then jerked the cock, marveling at the amount of clear pre-cum the man was oozing. He took the liquid and lubricated the cock with it, every vein and every fold of skin on the cock glistened in the lamp light. Orsinian rolled back, raised his legs in the air and exposed his ass. Maximus dropped to his knees and nuzzled his cock head in the opening. With Orsinian's legs on his shoulders, Maximus took hold of the Armenian's tits and began to play with them.

Maximus pushed in slowly, first only the tip of his head applied pressure to the hole, but didn't enter. Then the whole head popped in, up to the beginning of the shaft. The cock was oozing juice the entire time, lubricating both Maximus' cock and Orsinian's chute. He had not penetrated the sphincter yet. He then popped the head into the tunnel, just to the other side of the sphincter. He almost pulled it out and then eased in again.

During the match, Orsinian felt as if Badger's cock had ripped its way into his ass. Maximus' cock was exuding a soothing salve that took away the sharp pains of the earlier penetration. Maximus' cock was comfortable and enjoyable. As the cock went deeper and deeper, Orsinian became more excited.

Orsinian had always thought of being fucked as a professional obligation, a way to improve the show and earn more money. Unlike Cedric, he never took a cock except as part of the act. He was enjoying Maximus' slow pumping. As Orsinian relaxed, his ass opened more and Maximus went in deeper. The cock caused no pain, so the wrestler just laid back and enjoyed it.

Next to them, Cedric was still lowering and raising his ass on the ringed cock. It wasn't as exciting as he had thought it might be, but he realized it could be a long fuck; he wasn't going to shoot prematurely. He looked around the room and watched Otter, Hadrian and Orsinian squirming and moaning in pleasure as they fornicated. He knew Hadrian and Otter were fuck sluts, but he was surprised at Orsinian's obvious enjoyment.

Marcus' thin long cock didn't fill his hole so Cedric ground his ass in a circular movement forcing the cock to explore different parts of his rectum. He would pause and grind it when the cock hit a particularly enjoyable spot. He was always a considerate lover (except in the ring), and he watched Marcus to make sure he didn't miss an opportunity for pleasure.

"My god you're good!" Marcus exclaimed. "I thought Theo was good, but…" Marcus looked at the red haired bear with his bloated cock balancing on his thin cock. He was playing with Cedric's tits, and when Cedric arched his back, and rolled his eyes back in his head Marcus pinched the tender pink nipples.

"How long have you boys been playing together?" Cedric asked.

"I guess since we were born," he answered. "We were raised by our grandmother who was a demanding and austere woman. We had no toys, no games, only work and study. We found our own toys. At thirteen, we tried everything we could think of to stimulate ourselves. Our tutor once caught us at it, but he disliked our grandmother as much as we so he just joined in and gave us some pointers!" Marcus smiled with the reminiscence.

"Othacar taught us a lot too. We were quite isolated when we were boys. We were relieved to find out men like Othacar enjoyed the same things. He was a big and powerful man, we could reduce him to a quivering container of man seed," Marcus said. Cedric was beginning to have brief interludes of sexually induced shivering and as he continued to manipulate his ass around the ringed cock. For a big man Cedric was very limber, and he was all but doing a belly dance pivoting on Marcus' cock.

On the other side of the room, Otter's ass and Badger's cock were still oiled from the match, and Badger went deep on the first thrust. Otter gasped and his cock went ridged as a rock. Badger filled the hole and stretched the entire rectum with his oozing cock. Badger had watched Otter take Julian's cock many times, and had never seen him react with such obvious pleasure. Badger had never fucked an ass so responsive. Otter was trying to caress and massage Badger's cock, relaxing and tightening his muscles to manipulate the pumping organ.

Otter pushed Badger back and rolled up so he was sitting on Badger's cock. Otter then swung his legs around to try different positions pivoting his ass on Badger's cock. When Otter was facing away from Badger, and grinding his pelvic bone against the erect member, Badger moaned in pleasure. This movement rammed the underside of the erect cock head into Otter's prostate and it was as if the genitals of the two men had merged.

Arcturus and Optimus returned to the pool and relaxed. Julian joined them. Optimus realized he was the next man to take watch, so he got up and left to relieve Bembo of his duties. He put on a heavy cloak and went out into the storm.

"How are you doing?" Julian asked Arcturus. "Optimus is... filling."

"That's one way to put it!" Arcturus smiled.

"Was this the first time?" Julian asked.

"It sure was. I don't know if I want to do it again today, but I sure want to do it again soon." Arcturus confessed. Julian played with Arcturus' balls, and coaxed his cock to semi erection again. "Wolf took my load, but there must be more juice in the balls, I'm still excited."

"Well you started with the biggest cock in the villa, they only get smaller." Julian remarked. "Unless you get real lucky!" Julian smiled then told Arcturus about his interlude skewered on Optimus' cock.

Bembo entered the room. The warmth of the steamy room hit him, and he stripped and jumped into the pool. When he emerged, he joined Arcturus and Julian. "I must have missed quite a show." Bembo said. Julian told him of the nights events. Bembo was in the water at Arcturus' cock level so he took the half-erect member in his mouth.

"That's nice Bembo," Arcturus said, "But I think Julian was next in line."

"Don't worry," Julian said. "I can wait." He stood up, when Arcturus took his good arm and directed Julian's cock into his mouth. Julian had been uneasy as he had lost the exclusive use of the harem, and so far had only a sore ass from Optimus' fucking him as a replacement. As Arcturus began sucking him to full erection, Julian began to feel better about the entire situation. Arcturus wasn't as good as Fox, but he was obviously interested and vigorous. He suddenly felt his balls tightening. He held Arcturus' head back so only the cock head was in the mouth and slowed him. He also felt a itching in his ass and Julian realized he wanted to feel Arcturus' cock in his ass. He found himself remembering the moment when Optimus hit the magic nut, and wondered if Arcturus' cock would have the same effect. "I'm cumming!" he yelled. Arcturus greedily sucked in all the cream spewing from Julian's cock. He wouldn't let go of the ultra sensitive head. Julian twitched in ecstasy as the bear's rough tongue lapped at the head and tried to intercept the seed in the piss slit.

Julian's cry was enough to push all of the other men over the edge. Paulus pulled out of Hadrian and shot his load into the air, some landed in Hadrian' mouth, and he moaned as he shot off.

Otter exploded as he felt Badger's cum gushing into his ass. Cedric popped as he lost his balance and impaled himself on the ringed cock. Maximus pulled out of Orsinian, just as Orsinian shot load after load of white cum on his black pelt. Maximus added his own, then fell forward and kissed Orsinian, smearing sperm on their hairy chests and guts. Everyone had unloaded, except for Bembo, Fox and Arcturus.

Most of the men were exhausted and rolled onto the floor to rest and sleep. There was cum everywhere, dripping from the rapidly deflating cocks, on chests and legs. Bembo released Arcturus' cock and looked around. "What a mess!" he muttered.

Arcturus smiled and asked, "Are you going to clean it up?" He hadn't swallowed Julian's load, so it filled his mouth and dribbled onto his beard. Bembo looked at him and got excited by the man seed in Arcturus' beard. "Are you?" Arcturus asked again. Bembo rose up from the water and kissed Arcturus deep, tasting Julian's juice. "Let's clean them together." Arcturus suggested.

They went over to the sleeping forms of Maximus and Orsinian. Arcturus was going to start with Maximus' still dripping cock, but Bembo said, "He's mine." Arcturus began licking the cum from Orsinian's black pelt, lapped up all the cum, finding a deep pool in the navel, and aimlessly wondering if it was Orsinian's or Maximus' juice he was eating. When he was sucking the Armenian's cock he realized how he could identify the sperm and decided he would start with the cock of the next man. Fox had looked up from Wolf's cock, and decided to help out. He brought over a flagon of wine and the three men moved from man to man.

Arcturus worked on Badger next, while Fox and Bembo cleaned up Otter. Arcturus could taste the musky slime from Otter's ass mixed with the sweeter taste of Badger's pre-cum. He tried to deep throat Badger's impressive, half-erect cock, and was rewarded with a big shot of fresh cum. "Shit, Badger's still shooting!" he said. The cock disappeared in Arcturus' bearded mouth three more times and Badger twitched three more times.

Fox said, "Do it a couple of times more, he's almost done." Arcturus realized Fox's obsession with sucking had given him a good sense of how a man climaxed, and Badger was close to being finished. The next time he deep throated the cock, it had perceptibly shrunk.

It was early morning by the time they finished sucking and licking the other men clean. They sat together at the edge of the pool and took a final drink of wine. They looked at each other in the fading light of the lamps and laughed. The sperm of eight men clotted in their beards. Bembo returned to sucking Arcturus as the blond grant sucked Fox. Fox took Bembo's cock, and they formed a ring. Bembo popped first setting off a chain reaction.

No one swallowed so when the spasms stopped. They kissed and exchanged cum. Arcturus and Bembo fell asleep in each other's arms. Fox slept with Arcturus' cock in his mouth slowly sucking like a baby at a breast. All was quiet.

CHAPTER EIGHT

An Old Friend

The Twins, Fox and Badger were hunting in the early fall and they found another abandoned villa. This was not as rich as the seaside villas they had found before, and unlike the earlier ruins, this villa showed definite signs of having been re-occupied, and recently. Recent campfires and other signs showed that whoever had been there had made a hasty retreat. The twins knew enough from their stay in Germany to know this had been a Saxon camp.

They left behind German style cook pots and even a Saxon sword. This confirmed they had suffered a serious reversal and had fled. The men had Hellhound with them and the dog was interested but unconcerned with the place so they knew the Saxons weren't within smelling distance of the villa.

They spent the night nearby and continued the hunt the next day. Hellhound picked up a scent, and led the men on a race into the woods on the trail of game. Fox quickly realized something was wrong with the animal they were chasing. It was meandering through the woods, not moving in any particular direction. It was big and clumsy; broken branches marked its path. Blood stained some branches.

The dog suddenly barked. It had it. The three men raced to make the kill. Hellhound cornered a man. It was a big naked man, a big naked man with his eyes gouged out.

"Othacar!" Theo cried.

"Theodosius?" the man said in a strong German accent.

"What happened? How did you get here?" Theo looked at the badly beaten up man with no eyes. He called off the dog, and Fox and Badger looked on uneasily.

Theo talked to the man in German as the others consulted. "Let's kill him now, he's blind, he's of no use to anyone," Fox, who was always direct, stated.

Marcus looked genuinely shocked. "He saved our lives, and he is not Saxon, his tribe was the arch enemy of the Saxon swine"

"What in hell are we going to do with him?" Fox asked.

"I have no idea. But we'll take him, we'll find something for him to do," Marcus was usually mild mannered and quiet, he was agitated at the thought of killing Othacar, the man who had enslaved them.

Badger understood. The twins had spent a month fucking the German chieftain, trying to find some way to get their cocks in his ass without hurting him. From their description of the training they put him through; Othacar was in great pain the whole time. Unless he could take them both, all would have died. Badger guessed they had fallen in love with him. He was an impressive specimen, even in his beaten up state. Badger said, "Let's take him back and let the whole group decide."

"Kill me, put me out of misery! Death is better than this," Othacar cried in exceptionally bad Latin.

"The Twin God wants you alive," Theodosius stated. "And live you will. Marcus, you continue the hunt, I will take him back to the villa." Othacar smiled. The two groups separated.

Fox was muttering, "We can use his cock and his ass, but I don't know what we will do with the rest of him."

"Well, a cock and an ass are a start. And it is quite a cock," Badger remarked.

Theodosius led the man back to the villa stopping at a stream to clean the former chieftain up. There Othacar told him the story of his capture, enslavement and mutilation. Theo offered him some of the food he was carrying, Othacar wolfed it down, and Theo realized his request to die was not as genuine as it might have been.

Athgar had negotiated a peace treaty with the Saxons and Othacar, with his strongest men went to a banquet to celebrate the event. When they were all drunk, the Saxon's slaughtered them, all except Othacar who they enslaved, and Athgar, who they made chief of the tribe. Apparently Athgar was uneasy about having the beloved of Twin Oden killed.

They tortured him, beat him and mutilated him; poked his eyes out, and pierced his cock. When the Saxon's learned of the defeat, they left him alone and blind to die of starvation or exposure. At this point, Theo asked what they had done to him.

"Look yourself." Othacar replied. They were sitting on the bank of a stream, warmed by the autumn sun, and Theo took hold of Othacar's cock and peeled back the foreskin. It was a bloody mess inside.

"When did they do this to you?" Theo asked in a shocked voice.

"I don't know, I guess about a year ago. I can't figure time anymore." Othacar replied. "They put a new ring in maybe a month ago."

"Let me clean you up," Theo said as he began to wash the blood-caked head. Feeling his cock again brought back old feelings of affection and passion to Theo. He was going to complain to Othacar he should have cleaned it better. Then he realized he couldn't see. The chieftain had no way to know what it was like inside his foreskin. It took awhile, but Theo cleaned it all out. He looked at Othacar's purple cock head with a large rusted iron ring piercing the piss slit. The ring was much thicker than the twin's gold rings. Theo understood the ordeal.

"You know what it was like for us now," Theo said with a touch of bitterness.

"I wanted you to live. You were my only hope. You can't believe how hard it is to find twins with long, thin cocks," Othacar sounded desperate as he relived the search for the twins. "I wanted you to heal, not die of the puss in the wounds."

Theo put his arm around the blind man's shoulders and held him. He remembered the month of steady fucking had preceded the ritual, with Othacar wincing in pain every time they entered his ass. He also remembered the salves and potions that relieved the pain of the rings in their cocks. He remembered the excitement that accompanied the insertion of a new ring.

"Don't worry, all the gore in there was dried, you cock has healed. Does it still work?" Theo tweaked Othacar's tits.

"I really don't know," Othacar confessed, "I haven't used it in months."

"We will find out soon enough," said Theo, "Are you ready to go again?" The two men set off toward the villa.

Their arrival caused a stir. Maximus remarked to Optimus, the number of big, well-hung, hairy and naked men in the area was truly extraordinary. "Truly, God has blessed us," Optimus observed. The size of the group, both physical and genital had greatly expanded since they left the baths in the Roman city months ago.

Optimus went over to Othacar and took him away to attend to his wounds. He called in Julian to remove the ring. Othacar was frightened, since he had only a rudimentary understanding of Latin, and none of the educated Latin of Optimus. Optimus called in Theo who explained what they were doing.

They took him to the cold bath and cleaned up what Theo had missed in the stream, and then Optimus peeled back the skin exposing the ring. They took him outside. Optimus laid the cock on a smooth stone table, and Julian entered with a hammer and chisel. Theo thought they were lucky Othacar couldn't see. He would have thought they were going to castrate him.

"Stay still whatever happens!" Theo said. Julian placed the chisel on the ring and made a swift blow with the hammer. It went half way through the ring. The sound scared Othacar. His cock twitched due to the vibration. He was sweating profusely.

"Ready for another?" asked Julian. Theo translated and Othacar nodded. A third of the ring broke off. The edges were sharp so Julian went to get a file. He quickly returned and began filing the sharp edges. The vibration caused by the filing gave Othacar an erection. Theo watched the reaction of the men as they watched the horse cock enlarge. There was frank admiration. He had good length, but exceptional diameter. Otter drooled.

They returned to the cold pool and made Othacar stay in until he was completely chilled. The iron ring shrank a little, and Optimus removed it easily. They then went to the warm bath. The shivering blind man all but melted into the hot water. Bembo stayed with him.

Outside the men discussed the German chieftain. "Common sense says we should kill him," Hadrian said. "He is not one of us, and he is nothing but a liability. What can a blind man do?"

There was silence.

"Would it be murder?" asked Maximus.

"He has one hell of a cock," volunteered Otter. Everyone laughed, knowing Otter's interest and remembering the Twin's description of Othacar's interests.

"I have killed men in battle; I could execute a criminal, but I don't think I could kill a blind man," said Arcturus. That seemed to settle the question.

That night the hunters' returned and they had another feast. Othacar ate and fell asleep, waking in the middle of the night. Disoriented he moved and felt a body. Marcus asked, "Are you all right?" Othacar was relieved to hear a familiar voice.

"Yes, I need to piss," Othacar said, and Marcus helped him up and led him to the latrine. They stumbled over Wolf and Fox who were sleeping on the floor. "We're going to the latrine," whispered Marcus. The two men felt the same need so they all went to the facility.

The latrine was another marvel of hydraulics. It used the water from the pools to flush, and emptied the latrine over the cliff and into the sea. Othacar could hear the water crashing on the rocks below and hesitated. Marcus reassured him and Fox helped him aim.

Piss went everywhere. Some came out of the piss slit, some from the ring hole, and the foreskin trapped some and it dribbled. "What in hell is this?" Wolf cried as piss sprayed him. Othacar shook in humiliation.

"It's the second hole!" Fox said. Othacar didn't know what had happened. The ring had largely filled the second hole. It leaked before, but had never sprayed. "He can do nothing!" Othacar had held back for the entire day, and couldn't stop pissing.

Wolf reached over and held the shaking man. "Calm down. It's all right, finish it," Marcus translated. Wolf had dreaded the threat of genital mutilation, and felt pity for the blind man. They later learned the Saxons used Othacar as a latrine and he was terrified he would be punished and beaten.

It turned out Wolf and Fox's knowledge of obscene German matched Othacar's knowledge of vulgar Latin. "Let's clean up that fucker," Fox said as he went to a basin of warm water. He took a ladle of warm water poured it over Othacar's cock and splashed it on the floor. Wolf got a pail and cleaned the floor and seat. The water drained to concealed gutters and disappeared.

Fox lead Othacar to the basin and washed his cock. Wolf joined them, took Othacar's hands, and let his feel his own cock, "Wash mine!" Othacar relaxed some. Fox' hands explored the pierced cock as Othacar discovered Wolf's foreskin. "How long is that fuck pole?" he asked Wolf in his appalling Latin.

"When is the last time you shot some baby juice though your horse dick?" asked Fox in equally bad German. Othacar's cock began to thicken.

"Too long ago," moaned Othacar.

"Let me leave you to these boys," Marcus said in German, and in Latin, "Make him feel at home."

They led him to their sleeping place, and got him to lie down. Othacar didn't know what to expect, but suddenly a warm mouth enveloped his cock. A hand rubbed his hairy chest, stopping to feel his erect nipples. "Just relax, horse dick, and let nature take its course," Wolf whispered.

Fox was exploring the cock head, the cock was half-erect and he could work his tongue deep into the enlarged piss slit. The interior had healed, and while there were some hardened areas Fox guessed must be scars, most was tender with only a suggestion of the taste of urine.

Othacar had lived with the iron ring for months, a foreign body lodged in his cock. He had been relieved to have it removed earlier, but was unprepared to feel a living thing explore his penis, a warm living and wiggling thing. He could not believe the feeling. He was fully erect now, but Fox's tongue remained squeezed in the tube. Pre-cum bubbled up from his prostate and when Fox tasted it he redoubled his efforts to penetrate deeper into the tube. Othacar's had a big cock and also had a generously scaled sperm tube. Fox had his tongue inside the German's cock.

Fox pulled his tongue back, drawing the pre-cum into the entire shaft, and then tried to force his tongue back deeper into the slit. The engorged cock made this difficult, but the battle between the cock and the tongue was enjoyable for both men. Othacar was a fucker, not a sucker, but passion and excitement overwhelmed him. No man had taken is whole cock in the mouth, but Fox did it effortlessly. Othacar felt the urge to suck cock, and Wolf seemed to understand and fed him his meat.

Othacar expected the acrid taste of urine. His captors made sure he knew about this. He got the sweet taste of pre-cum. He had always screwed his own men in the steam room, and the filthy habits of the Saxons sickened him. He loved Wolf's cock; the cock head lubricated the inside of the skin with pre-cum, refreshing it every time he licked the knob.

Fox could feel Othacar tense up, and then the first empty twitches. Fox had time to wedge his tongue into the tube and intercept the flow. He felt sperm tickle his tongue as it tried to find an outlet. It was briefly trapped in the convulsing cock. Then came the flood.

Fox realized this was a once in a lifetime load. Othacar hadn't shot off in months. He filled Fox's mouth. Fox swallowed it and then the pulsing cock filled it again. Wolf pulled his cock out of Othacar's mouth so he could breathe. Othacar kept on twitching and shooting, Fox was in heaven. Finally Othacar stopped shooting and twitching, he felt drained. Yet Fox knew there was more cum stored in the balls and kept sucking and licking. The blind man had a long night ahead of him.

At dawn Fox woke and licked the cock next to his mouth. Othacar was still asleep and his cock was soft. He worked his tongue into the gaping hole vacated by the ring on the underside of the penis. His tongue fit and Fox began working it into the cock toward the head. The soft cock allowed easy entrance and deep penetration. Wolf watched as the tongue's stimulation affected the sleeping man's cock. As it began to engorge, the skin pulled back exposing Othacar's monumental cock head and the enlarged piss slit.

Wolf was fascinated as the piss slit began to open, and he saw Fox's tongue inside the slit, working its way out. Othacar was awake now and trying to figure out what he felt in his horse cock. Wolf took the entire head into his mouth, jammed his tongue into the slit and Fox and Wolf's tongues met in at the base of Othacar's cock head.

Othacar was in heaven, as his cock grew and hardened, it forced the two tongues out of his throbbing member. Fox lost the battle first, but Wolf continued to force his tongue deep. Othacar climaxed with all of the juice dribbling out of the ring hole. Wolf was not interested in cum, and this was the first time he had felt a man have a dry climax. Fox got the sperm, Wolf sucked the ultra sensitive cock head, Othacar couldn't figure out what was happening to him, but couldn't have enjoyed it more.

That morning Othacar became a member of the group. As Badger had said, a cock and an ass were a start. Both Wolf and Fox, the most negative members of the group, now liked the blind man. Maximus and Optimus worked to extend his Latin vocabulary. Optimus commented while in this collection of men, donkey dong and fuck pole were useful words, a more utilitarian vocabulary might be in order.

Othacar was an intelligent man, and picked up the language quickly. He had been made the chieftain because of his cock, and didn't mind being fondled or played with by whoever was passing. He soon recognized the voices and personalities of the men in the group. He regained his strength quickly, and helped Cedric and Orsinian with their construction work.

Most importantly, he told them of the Saxon's plans for the next year's attacks. Since he had been blind and a slave, they had not tried to conceal their plans from him and had openly discussed the next wave of the invasion and their objectives. Theodosius translated all to Arcturus. Arcturus began to plan.

Othacar and his cock also inspired some planning. His horse cock was big and the mutilation had made it unusual, and Othacar himself was as interested in it and its recreational potential as any of the men in the group. He was more than willing to see how much fun for him and his new friends it could provide.

They needed to solve some technical problems such as how to keep him from pissing all over the place every time he took a leak. Optimus had the educated Roman's interest in hydraulics, but couldn't figure out what direction the urine would emerge from the German's cock. An old flagon of wine, with a big belly and constricted neck solved the problem. Othacar's wine became the subject of considerable mirth.

The piss tube between the ring hole and the cock head dried out since it wasn't used for piss, pre-cum or cum any more. Hadrian soaked a strip of cloth in salve and worked it into the hole and out the head. This lubricated the tube and excited Othacar too. Soft rawhide worked the same way. His huge dong with the laces of rawhide hanging from the foreskin was curiously exciting. His cock would be soft and relaxed until someone pulled the string. Fox said it looked good enough to eat, and Maximus took this as an invitation to create a new culinary delight.

Maximus suggested a new treat to Othacar who was game. Some meat, especially venison was tough and stringy. Maximus, marinated it, cooked it and cut it into long strips. After dipping it in oil and cooling it, he worked it into the cock, so only the tip of the meat was visible in the slit.

He selected Fox as the taste tester. In the early afternoon when most of the men were working Maximus got Wolf to tell Fox that Othacar need to get off. Fox was happy to oblige and found Othacar in the thermal pool. Maximus and Wolf watched the two men meet, kiss and Fox slowly dropped to his knees. Maximus was surprised at the tenderness Fox showed toward Maximus.

Fox began to work on the cock, and he quickly got Othacar erect and the skin retracted. He tasted the meat before he saw it. He pulled back and looked curiously at the venison peaking out of the cock head, and then looked over at Maximus and Wolf who were laughing. "Eat it!" Wolf cried. Eat it he did.

You couldn't tell who enjoyed it more, Fox, Othacar or the two observers. The meat was well seasoned but tough. Fox would nibble at it, and then chew it, and then had to suck like hell to draw the next bit of meat from the tube. Othacar moaned in pleasure as Fox slowly pulled the meat through his cock and devoured it. Othacar was so hard; the meat was all but wedged in the tube testing Fox's sucking skills to their limits. When he finished the meat, Fox tongued the seasoned inside of the chute then deep throated the entire cock. Othacar's balls provided the final special sauce. Wolf touched Fox's cock to see how much he had like the meal and was instantly covered with shooting sperm. One touch was enough to push Fox over the edge.

"Did you like it?" Wolf asked.

"Shit yes!" replied the ever articulate Fox. Othacar shot another load of cum in response.

As the men calmed down, Maximus suggested they keep this new taste treat a secret among themselves for a while. He wanted it to be a feature of a festive event. They all agreed.

CHAPTER NINE

New Skills

Maximus and Optimus were talking on the windswept terrace overlooking the sea. "I guess we could go back to Verulamium and see what's left," observed Maximus. "Othacar's report seems to confirm earlier reports. I should be safe now."

"Why? What's in it for us?" Optimus said. "It's a lot of work here, and we may be more exposed than inland, but I don't think I could leave."

"So many cocks and ass holes, so little time?" Maximus smiled.

"You read my mind. Cedric told me you had quite a glow on the other night as you taught Orsinian to take it in the ass. You connected."

"I was just being polite and helpful," Maximus admitted, "and suddenly I felt Orsinian come alive. He turned into the mass of cum like the way the twins described Othacar. I was interested scientifically, of course, and then found myself converting to sperm too. How many times have I fucked you? I never felt anything like it."

"I know what you mean. My visit to his ass was fun, and I loved my stint as the Eastern Queen, but Wolf excites me. That hairy animal drives me crazy. I was almost as excited telling Arcturus what to do and watching him experience Wolf's cock, as when I did it myself," Optimus admitted.

Dusk was falling; a cold wind blew from the sea. Paulus joined them. "We were talking about how much we enjoy this place, and these men," Optimus said. Paulus wore only a light tunic, and Maximus invited him into his warm, heavy cloak, Optimus joined them forming a tent with the two cloaks.

"I feel like I had died and been born again," Paulus said. "Years of no friends, little shelter and almost no food, then I run into the bears, and a few days later the rest of you."

"You have made us happy. Hadrian is ready to adopt you and leave you his worldly fortune! That was quite a show you put on!" Maximus said.

"Hadrian is a good teacher, very patient too. I fucked Cedric because he wanted it and I was afraid they might leave me if I didn't. After all those years I was desperate for some protection. I'd have let them fuck me if they wanted. Hadrian was fun," Paulus said.

"Hadrian I am sure can be very patient with a cock like yours in his ass," observed Maximus. "I bet he learned a few things too."

Paulus blushed. "Maybe, but he is very nice. I talked to Cedric and Orsinian to see if they were unhappy with me for being with another man. They said we aren't married, we are just helping out, and there is enough cock here for everybody." As the discussion turned to cocks, the three men realized it was warm inside the cloaks and the temperature was not the only thing rising. "I talked to them about another problem…" He hesitated. "I've never had a cock in my ass."

"That shouldn't be a problem here," laughed Optimus. "No problem at all."

"I guessed that! The problem is, everything is so open here, and I want to know what it feels like before the whole group sees me. I am not really interested in being fucked, except…" continued Paulus.

"Except?" asked Optimus.

"Well, except when I was fucking Cedric and Hadrian. I really wanted something in my ass," Paulus said. "When I get really hot Orsinian said I should talk to you, you are an easy first fuck." He said indicating Maximus. Maximus was inwardly flattered at Orsinian's comments, he was erect, and he could feel Paulus' cock slowly pumping on his leg.

"I can tell you Max is good," Optimus said, "and that is from years of experience. Should I leave? Maybe I should just bend over the terrace wall and look away." Optimus did this.

Paulus was a good student and realized Optimus' hole was open and at cock height as he bent over the wall. He nuzzled the cock head in the hole and applied pressure, tying to do what Orsinian had said Maximus had done. The cold wind, a warm body and the hot hole did the trick.

After a few dozen short pumping movements, the head was well in. Optimus was growling a low tone. "Ram him, He doesn't mind!" Maximus said. Paulus obeyed and Optimus let out a quivering moan. "Don't be afraid to go deep." Maximus knew the insides of Optimus' rectum well and knew the feelings Paulus was experiencing. "Tell me when you have an empty feeling inside your ass!" His cock was oozing buckets and Maximus positioned his thick cock head at Paulus' hole, filling it with lube. "My cock is thick, so you might be better off with Fox or Wolf."

"Now! I'm ready now!" Paulus whispered. Paulus had spread his legs to apply more pressure to his cock as he fucked Optimus. His hole was wide open. The head cleared the sphincter on the first nudge. Paulus reached back, grabbed Maximus' ass and impaled himself on the cock in one movement.

The ass was tight, but immediately relaxed as Maximus' pubic hairs touched the ass. Maximus realized the cock head must have rammed the magic nut on the first thrust. "You like it don't you?" he asked. From Optimus' growling Maximus knew his former lover's prostate was getting a work out.

"Incredible! Paulus gasped.

"Hold back a little!" Maximus asked.

"Shit no." Paulus cried as he buried his spewing cock deep in the ass. Optimus tried to wiggle his ass a bit, but the boy's cock was at full inflation, and there was no room in his ass for anything but sperm.

Paulus collapsed over Optimus' back like a wet blanket and all of his incredible sexual energy drained from his cock into the warm ass. Maximus stopped pumping. Relaxing, he let his cock shrink in Paulus' hole. He was afraid once the intense sexual feeling diminished, the boy might begin the feel the pain from the impaling.

"I thought I wouldn't like it," whispered the young man. His cock was now free of the ass and dripped sperm on the stone pavement.

"You aren't going to become another Otter are you?" Maximus asked as he gave a pump or two with his semi erect cock, still stretching the hole.

"I understand it now. It was great. I couldn't understand what Cedric, Otter and Hadrian were so interested in," Paulus said. "It takes your breath away."

"It's a lucky man who can enjoy so much so fast. Otter must have an ass built for fun. Maybe his nut is the size of an apple. You need to talk to Cedric, he has firsthand experience with it," Optimus said. He realized he wanted to feel Otter's insides, and find out why Otter was the way he was.

"I once thought the man on top was the real man and the man below feminine. The real man is the one who knows what he wants, and is willing to help anyone who can help him. You can't be more masculine than Cedric, even when he is bouncing on a cock!" observed Optimus. "I also thought this was an interest of over educated men, trying to emulate the Greek fashion."

"Well you can't get less educated the Wolf or Otter!" Paulus interjected. Maximus' was no longer in his ass. "I'm sorry, but I need to go in, I'm freezing!" They let him out of the cloak, and he ran toward the warm subterranean rooms of the villa. As he left, Orsinian walked up.

"You helped my friend with is little problem?" he asked.

"I sure did, thanks for the recommendation," Maximus replied.

"He enjoyed it?"

"No problem, he knows a lot more about himself than he did. At least the anatomy of his ass," Optimus reassured the man. "And something about mine too, he is a good fucker."

"I thought he would like it, Cedric was his first fuck, and he took to it like a duck to water," Orsinian said. "He's a good boy and we wanted him to like it. Did he shoot?

"Oh yes, but a bit too fast for our pleasure I think it would have been a sight to behold if he hadn't been buried so deep in my friend's ass," answered Maximus. "I'm sure once he gets some practice he will be able to screw Hadrian and take it for hours. He's a fast learner."

"Thanks again," said Orsinian, "If you still have full loads, come and see me after dinner. We can play." It was getting very cold by then and they all walked back to the villa.

Sleeping arrangements remained informal inside the villa. The twins always slept together, they fucked each other all of the time and couldn't seem to sleep without a bit of cock play. The rest of the men slept wherever they were. Those who liked it warm gravitated to the stone benches around the thermal pool. The hunters and the bears liked the cooler central hall, or even the edge of the chilly, cold spring. The festive wrestling nights or story nights took place once or twice a week, but most of the time the heavy physical labor demanded by their life encouraged most of the men to sleep. Most slept heavily. The combination of work, good food and some wine insured sleep. Thus while everyone enjoyed sexual play, by the time it got dark most needed to sleep.

On a normal night, there were few lamps burning, oil was difficult to make and Hadrian was always frugal, so there was some privacy. One on one sessions occurred sporadically. All of the men made use of the baths, since they were natural there was no need to maintain them and they operated all day and all night.

At the entrance to the bath there was a hook holding rawhide laces. Originally they were to bind the foreskin over the head in the Greek fashion. Greek athletes were only naked if the cock head was exposed, and this insured modesty. Here it was an informal indication you were interested in some play. You would wrap it around your cock and balls. This would display your cock to advantage, and if you did it tightly enough, leave you semi erect. It wasn't a rule, or even stated, so there was no problem if you went in for a good soaking and ended up with a mouth full of cum, but it simplified life.

They all understood that, other than on festive nights, sex was one on one, or by invitation only. Everywhere except in the thermal pool, the rawhide tie was an open invitation to all. The only restriction was all sexual activity had to be voluntary. Julian liked a certain level of control, and was a bit unhappy. Arcturus, Optimus and Othacar regarded sex as an expression of rank and power, but in this group, none of them had any interest in expressing themselves that way.

Later, Maximus and Optimus quietly talked in the thermal pool, sitting on the marble platform ringing the room. There was only one lamp. Someone came in the room, stopped at the door and then jumped into the pool. He played in the pool for a short while. He got out and came over to the two men. "Greetings! I'm glad you're here," Orsinian said.

"Come join us," Optimus said. He patted the seat next to him and the Armenian sat. The rawhide tie was difficult to see in the dark room, partially concealed in the thick black hair, but it was there. Orsinian had no trouble seeing the ties on the other men's cocks. "We are solving the problems of the world."

"I may not be able to help you with the world, but if there is anything closer at hand I can do please don't hesitate," Orsinian sat down. He didn't know how Optimus had reacted to the obvious pleasure he had experienced earlier on his lover's cock. Optimus put is arms on his shoulders and pulled him nearer.

"We were commenting on this remarkable collection of men. It's hard to believe we could all end up in the same place with such similar interests and likes," Maximus said. "No one seems to be a problem."

"Everyone likes cock," interjected Optimus. Two more men entered the room and got into the pool sighing in pleasure as their bodies felt the warm bubbly water.

"A few months ago I was running for my life, today I am sitting in a heated pool in the middle of the night watching the lamplight reflect from a huge cock. Is that sweat or pre-cum giving it that shine?" Orsinian said.

"You are a philosopher," Maximus said. All laughed. "I think you need to taste it to know." Orsinian got on his knees and began to suck Optimus' cock. "But it is hard to know what the future will bring. Saxons I am afraid."

From the pool a voice said, "Dead Saxons, if I have anything to do with it." It was Arcturus. Orsinian was having trouble deep throating the massive dong, so Optimus directed him to Maximus' cock. He attacked it with enthusiasm. Optimus could feel the excitement rise in the two men.

"We are only sixteen men; do we have a chance against the Germans?" Optimus asked.

"With Othacar's information we do. We have a chance at least," Arcturus said. Optimus made Orsinian lie down next to him with his head in his lap and directed Maximus to get into position. As Maximus raised the Armenian's legs to open up the hole, Optimus felt the excitement build. Arcturus got out of the pool, with his companion, Julian, and came over to watch. Maximus and Orsinian were in a different world as their genitals slowly merged.

Julian was half-erect and Arcturus was hard. "I would love to try it," Arcturus said. "I've never fucked a man." Optimus watched as Julian's meat expanded, and wondered if it would shoot now or just explode.

"Be my guest," Optimus said with a grin. "I have a souvenir of Paulus' seed in my ass, but that will lubricate you well!" He watched as Julian turned red.

"You don't want a used hole for your first fuck! My ass is virgin," Julian looked at the other men as he said this, and amended. "More virgin than his." Optimus laughed.

"He may not be virgin, but he is tight! Optimus said. Maximus and Orsinian had calmed down and were now slow fucking. They had reached a level of high excitement, but had no drive to cum, so they both enjoyed the ride. Optimus left them alone.

Arcturus embraced Julian, and they were grinding their cocks together. "Break it up," Optimus demanded. Optimus was sitting down and he grabbed the men's balls and pulled them close. "I thought you wanted to fuck." From their balls he worked a finger back and now explored each man's ass. He went right for the prostate and pushed, Arcturus and Julian were in his control.

"God yes, I want to fuck!" Arcturus said as he tried to get more of the finger into his prostate.

Julian couldn't talk as waves of excitement spread from his ass.

"Would you like a lesson?" Optimus asked Arcturus. He nodded and Optimus began to suck the bear's cock as he fingered the hole. It was rock hard, and he realized he couldn't suck for long before he shot. He released the cock and concentrated on Julian. "How do you like it?" Julian's prostate was deep, and his long finger could barely reach it. It obviously was tender.

"Doggy style," Julian whispered. Optimus stood up and then lifted Julian up, with one hand holding the chest, and one gripping the asshole, then lowered him to the floor. Julian's hole was wide open and Arcturus needed no more invitation. His dripping cock head was in the twitching ass.

"Do you want it fast or slow?" Optimus asked Arcturus.

"I want it to last," Arcturus said.

"Then work it in real slow." Optimus got some oils and dripped it on Arcturus' meat. The head was already in the hole, but he pulled it out so Optimus could lubricate it. Optimus sat on the floor with his cock in Julian's face and made him suck it. This forced him to open is ass more. Julian was whimpering. Whimpering and moaning in pleasure. When half of the donkey dong was in, it hit the prostate and Julian moaned and deep throated all of Optimus' cock. Arcturus watched and guessed this was a good time to go deep. He guessed right, Julian almost came.

"Pull it all the way out then push it in all the way," Julian asked. He moaned on every penetration. After thirty or forty thrusts, he asked, "Can you pull out and rest for a bit, I can't take it anymore?"

"Shit I could do this for hours," Arcturus said, but he pulled out anyway. "You are tight!"

Optimus had sat up on the bench again, "Would you like to try another ass?"

Arcturus looked at Julian and asked, "Do you mind?"

"Just save your load for me," Julian replied. Arcturus went over to Optimus lifted his legs in the air and entered. His cock was greased with oil and pre-cum; Optimus was still filled with Paulus' load, so it was a very easy entry.

"Whoa! You are open!" Arcturus exclaimed. "Nice and easy. Nice and warm." He was pumping at an easy rate and Optimus began to tighten his chute as Arcturus pulled out. "My god what are you doing?" Arcturus gasped.

"Milking," Optimus said.

"It's my turn now!" Julian reconsidered his generosity in allowing Arcturus to fuck Optimus. Arcturus returned to Julian and deep dicked him. His ass was relaxed and all thought and memory of pain was gone.

Optimus was relaxing on the bench, still savoring Arcturus' fuck when he felt something splatter on his chest. He looked and saw Arcturus shooting. He came while pulling out of Julian, shot sperm over the blacksmith, and hit him in the first volley. It was the third or fourth shot landed on Julian's back,

"I wanted it," Julian said, he felt disappointment and then a cock filled his ass again and he moaned in pleasure.

"Your ass is a lot hotter tonight." Julian herd Optimus speak from behind. Julian recalled the first time Optimus fucked him and was going to tell him to pull out. Instead he said," Go deeper and faster, I've got to cum!"

Optimus slowed down. "Beg a little more!" he said.

"Pump harder, all that cum is trapped, I can't get it to release," Julian whined. Please. "Harder faster!"

"Arcturus, watch this baby cry," Optimus said, "Come over here and give him something to teeth on." Arcturus came over and fed his slimy cock, covered in pre-cum, Paulus' cum and ass scum. Julian gobbled it up. Optimus leaned over the man, pinched his small erect nipples, and finally began to pump hard. He rammed the ass over and over again. He climaxed in a whole body ejaculation. He felt as if every fluid in his body was trying to get into his balls and then into Julian's twitching ass. Arcturus was stroking Julian's cock as Julian sucked him off and got a handful of cum. It felt like Julian was taking a long piss, but it was all milky man juice. It filled Arcturus big paw and the overflowed onto the floor. "You fuckers!" Julian said.

"Complaining?" Optimus asked.

Arcturus lifted Julian up from the doggy position, and offered his cum covered hand to him to lick. Julian lapped it up. "Is that all mine?" he asked.

"It sure is!" Arcturus answered as he wiped the gobs of cum onto Julian's beard. Optimus cleaned Arcturus' juice from his chest and added it to Julian's beard. The three men kissed and licked. Optimus would take a gob of cum on his tongue and offered it to the other men who would playfully fight over the drop of sperm.

Next to them Maximus and Orsinian slept. They had quietly climaxed while the others fucked. Everyone slept.

CHAPTER TEN

Plans

Cold weather arrived early along with massive storms. Arcturus, Maximus and Othacar worked at planning the defense against the expected Saxon onslaught. The hunters in the group scouted out the entire area and Othacar had a superb memory. He had surveyed the entire area before they blinded him. Othacar was aware of the outline of their plans. Maximus was knowledgeable about military tactics. They soon concluded they would need more men if they were to turn the Saxons back at the beach.

Arcturus volunteered to recruit more men. He was the only man in the group with local connections. He was from a prominent family and his in-laws were equally important. Arcturus felt his in laws were the most likely source of men and he would travel to see them. He selected Bembo, Orsinian, Badger and Paulus to accompany him. A leader needed an entourage to be credible. The muscle men provided the beef, Paulus had a noble name, and Badger was a scout. They would look formidable and impressive, but the success of the recruiting expedition was not assured. All Britain was dangerous, and whether anyone would leave their tribes to undertake an attack on the Saxons was uncertain. Men might ambush them and turn their severed heads over to the Saxons for a reward.

Maximus and Julian would continue to organize the defenses of the villa itself. Everyone could fight except Othacar, and he could look impressive as long as no one knew he was blind. Julian made weapons, and Arcturus was pleased the blacksmith had a gift for fine swords and spears. He made beautiful and strong weapons. They were also fearsome looking. Fantastical dragons and snakes populated his swords and pikes. Arcturus knew the dragons did nothing for the killing ability of the sword, but they instilled confidence in the men who used them. The legions of Rome had defended the island for centuries. The civilian soldiers needed all the confidence they could get when they faced the barbarian Saxons.

Hadrian was not going to let the recruiting party to set off on their dangerous task without a celebration. He planned a major event for the eve of the departure. In the morning as the sun rose Maximus lead an impressive service asking for God's blessing on the expedition, invoking the aid of the Father, Son and Holy Spirits, the Blessed Mother of God and all the saints and martyrs. He christened Bembo as Joshua, the warrior. Othacar converted and Maximus baptized him as Samson, the blind hero. The general theme of the service was to destroy our enemies and crush their bones into dust. All knew Maximus was sending his lover Orsinian off on a dangerous mission. Genuinely moved, his words were not empty, but mighty invocations to God.

That night there was a banquet with plentiful food and wine. The twins stood watch with the dogs and they sealed the doors. Hadrian had all the lamps burning. There were toasts and speeches. Optimus began with a tribute to brotherhood and manly love. Hadrian praised protecting friends. Julian added a touching toast to men with big cocks who knew how to use them. Arcturus surprised everyone by giving thanks to the Heavens for the prostate, and giving all men a way to reach it. It was a jovial event and everyone was feeling good

Maximus then stood, "Friends! For this special occasion Otha... I mean Sampson and I have developed a special desert for you all. Marinated venison, a rare delicacy..." he held up a string of meat, "and served as only Sampson can. He wants to personally serve you, one and all!" Sampson got up, walked toward Maximus, and dropped his loincloth. He was semi-erect. As always, his huge member attracted the attention and few noticed the piece of meat hanging to his knees from the ring hole. He then peeled back the foreskin and exposed the meat protruding through his piss slit. The room burst into rowdy laughter.

"Eat hardily my friends!" Sampson bellowed. Arcturus jumped up, dropped to his knees, grabbed the meat between his teeth, and pulled a finger's length through the cock. Sampson cried "Oh baby!" and the festivities began. Arcturus bit off some meat, swallowed it, and then deep throated the cock. Soon, Badger worked his way between the men and dislodged Arcturus and pulled another length through the German's pierced horse cock. By the end of the night, everyone in the room had a taste of what Optimus called meat wrapped in meat. The newly renamed Sampson had an incredible sex drive and the stamina of a workhorse. He never tired.

He had served about half the men when the first ribbon of meat was gone. There was no way to get another serving into his bloated cock until he calmed down and his erection subsided. The men who had been most excited had already tasted him. Some of the others had gotten desert from other sources. Optimus' tongue was deep inside Wolf's skin. Joshua was serving Maximus his cock.

Orsinian stood and shouted. "Wrestling Time!" The men applauded and hooted as the group wondered what the wrestlers had in store for them this time. The first match was between Cedric and Orsinian. This turned out to be a conventional wrestling match. Both men were superb athletes and great wrestlers, and the men watching began rooting for one or the other, caught up in the bout. Their previous matches had been sexual games done for entertainment. Most didn't realize Cedric and Orsinian were serious wrestlers.

It also gave everyone a chance to calm down. Hadrian had planned the night as he had planned many parties in the houses he served in the past. He realized if you had the climax too soon the night would be a disappointment. He also knew if the men could subside a bit after the high of Sampson's performance, they could go a lot longer before they would cum. Hadrian wanted it to be a long night.

The match went for three rounds and the crowd declared it a draw. Both men had clearly given it their all. Arcturus was glad Orsinian was coming with him. A strong man would impress the men they needed to recruit. Hadrian served wine to all.

"And for the Second event in tonight's games we have the Old Testament Hero from Germany versus Cedric the British Bruin." Orsinian cried. Everyone was briefly puzzled, and then realized Sampson was not done for the night.

Cedric had talked about this with Othacar-Sampson weeks earlier, and the blind man was interested. Blindfolded matches were common wrestling events, often done as a filler between major matches. Usually they pitted a huge, professional, blindfolded wrestler against a small man who could see. They did the matches for comic effect. Sampson had wrestled many men as a youth asserting his right to be a chieftain. He was good at it, and wanted to try again.

Cedric saw the man was interested, but was holding back. "What's the problem?" he asked quietly.

Sampson whispered. "I don't like to be fucked much. Your big cock would rip me to pieces." While he was well endowed, Cedric was average in this group of men, and Sampson's judgment pleased him.

"Frankly, I have been thinking about your cock in my ass ever since Julian filed off the ring and I saw your boner. There is no way I would let you lose. I will even use a real blindfold," Cedric said.

"You like to be fucked?"

"Love it, and I like 'em big," Cedric answered. "We are agreed?"

Sampson agreed, and they began some secret practice sessions. Cedric knew all the tricks and the German learned quickly. The blind man didn't want to look like a fool, but didn't mind a comedy routine and had no objection to sex in public at all. He had been doing for years in the steam baths at his home.

The match was a great success. They were naked of course, with their bodies glistening with sweat. Both cocks were oiled, but the onlookers couldn't tell it wasn't sweat, and Cedric's ass was thoroughly lubricated. Cedric did not use a real blindfold, he could see and he insured the tricks worked.

They started grappling, with Sampson's free arm grasping at air and just happening to capture Cedric's cock. Cedric grabbed Sampson's leg and pulled it out, dropping him to the floor with a loud, but painless thud. Sampson rolled him over and they reversed positions. They ended up with their mouths next to the other man's cocks and both took a lick. The room filled with a roar of approval and laughter. "Pin him, don't suck him!" Otter yelled.

Maximus refereed as usual and called an end to the round. In the second round, Sampson grabbed Cedric by the crotch and then lifted him over his head. He rotated him around so all could see as Cedric cried piteously to let him down. No one realized how strong the German was, and there were sounds of admiration. As he lowered Cedric his thumb just happened to slip into Cedric's ass, and Cedric began twitching the way Otter did when Orsinian fingered him.

Cedric was making everything work out just right, and was well satisfied with the performance when Sampson applied a lot more pressure to Cedric's magic nut than he had at the practice sessions. Cedric went limp with the uncontrollable feelings emanating from his ass. He was afraid Sampson might forget what he needed to do and they might get hurt. He could not say anything. His mouth was open making a silent moan of pleasure.

Sampson lowered Cedric to the floor, rolled him on his back, shoved his cock into the deepest recesses of Cedric's rectum and pinned him. After the thumb's unbearable pressure on his prostate, the horse cock was a relief. Cedric screamed, "Damn that's good!" Sampson began pumping.

"Break it up. The match is over!" Maximus demanded.

Sampson pulled out. "I'll finish this later!" he said.

They left the room for the cold spring and cleaned up. "Are you all right?" Sampson asked.

"I will be some day. You will finish fucking me?" Cedric asked.

"I think I could spend a lot of time fucking you," Sampson said. The two men kissed. When the two men entered the main room again, Sampson peeled back the foreskin again revealing a new piece of meat threaded through his cock. The room burst into applause.

Joshua, Badger, Arcturus and Otter made up the third match. The two smaller men climbed on the shoulders of the bigger men. The objective was to dismount the man who was riding. Again, the strength of the men astonished all. Badger and Otter weren't big men, but they were men, and neither Joshua nor Arcturus showed any signs of discomfort with their loads.

They also didn't mind having the two, smaller men humping their necks as they grappled above. At one time Joshua dropped to his knees and began sucking Arcturus as Badger tried to dislodge Otter. Joshua rose again without any assistance. Badger and Otter were naturally competitive and they tried to win. They would get into a clutch and Arcturus, who was taller than Joshua, would lick Badger's swollen cock head as it peaked from behind Joshua's neck. Both men were able to suck the other's partner at one time.

The contrast between the feisty top men and their cock sucking mounts was amusing and enjoyable. Badger and Otter were battling fiercely, but also were erect, their mounts were semi erect, but had an affectionate and clearly sexual relationship. The first round was a draw.

"For the second round, we're going to make this a bit more difficult. They will trade partners," Orsinian announced. "They will do it blind." Everyone expected this to be a rehash of Sampson and Cedric's match. The four men entered as they had before, but Badger and Otter climbed on their partner's shoulders facing in the other direction. Their cocks were in Arcturus and Joshua's faces not the backs of their heads. There were more ribald comments and cheers.

Neither of the mounts could see beyond their partners' pubic hair. Arcturus enjoyed the chance to see Badger's impressive meat up close. The sweat dripping from the diminutive, hair-covered man added to the attraction. He licked Badger's balls then sucked them into his mouth. Joshua had never felt an interest in Otter, but the musky smell of Otter's genitals pressed against his mouth and nose and the rivulets of fresh sweat pouring from Otter's body affected him. Desire began to build. He licked at the balls and got increasingly excited.

All four men fell down simultaneously and they declared the match a draw. After the match, the entire group adjourned to the thermal pool to cool down and clean up.

Paulus timidly came up to Sampson, touched him on the shoulder and asked, "Can I have some?" there was part of a meat strip threaded through Sampson's cock.

"Is there any left?" Sampson asked.

"About a hand's length," The boy answered. "Are you the last?" the German asked.

"I think so." Sampson said, "Finish it up boy!" and under his breath he asked, "And when you are done could you clean out the chute? It's getting a bit tender."

Sampson sat on the bench and opened his legs; Paulus dropped to his knees. He grabbed the venison with his teeth and pulled. Sampson moaned again. Twelve men had sucked him so far and Sampson was still hard and ready to go. The young father less boy tenderly and slowly drew the last piece of meat through the holes, periodically deep throating the horse dick.

"You'd better hold off on that if you want to get into the piss tunnel, you can't get in if it's too hard," Sampson said. Paulus complied and the two men relaxed and talked.

"Do you have sons?" Paulus asked.

"Three. But I don't know if they are still alive," Sampson answered. "I don't know how many of my family the Saxon's killed when they captured me." Paulus told him the story of his father's death and the destruction of his family. Sampson was sympathetic, but had a difficult time understanding, since his grasp of Latin was inadequate to understand Paulus' cultured speech. He got the drift and asked Paulus to kill a Saxon for him. Their mutual losses bound them together. Paulus looked down and realized the effort to understand him had distracted Sampson, and the giant cock was flaccid.

Paulus immediately deep throated the cock and worked his tongue deep in the hole. He was tall and thin, his tongue was long and thin, and he penetrated deeper than anyone had before, even Fox.

Sampson moaned in pleasure and sighed in relief as the soothing tongue cleaned the inside of the sperm channel. Maximus walked by and patted Sampson. He asked how he was doing.

"Great," Sampson answered, "But less pepper next time!" Both smiled. Paulus was excited as the spicy insides of the cock quivered and grew harder. The very tip of his tongue tasted the sweet man juice Sampson was producing again. Thirteen men had sucked him. Sampson had fucked Cedric. Now the German giant was ready to rejoin the action.

It was quiet and relaxed as the men soaked in the pool or on the marble bench. All knew this might be the last time they ever saw each other alive. The times were uncertain and death was everywhere. This was the last time they might share each other company, love or lust. As men, they were all embarrassed to express love verbally; men just didn't do that, but they all had cocks, erect cocks.

Julian went over to Badger whispered in his ear. Julian went to the bench, rolled back pulled his knees to his chest and exposed his hole. Badger spit on his hand, coated his cock and fucked to the hilt. Few knew Arcturus had broken in Julian, and they were surprised when Julian moaned and began to beg for more deep thrusts. It was the first time any member of the harem had been in his former master's ass and everyone's dick stiffened. Fox came over and fed Julian his cock while he kissed Badger.

Paulus was still sucking Sampson's dick next to them. The German's organ was ridged and sticking straight up by then. Paulus got up, straddled the cock, and sat on it. An incredible look of satisfaction spread over the blind man, it was as if he could see again. He was a man again. Paulus tried to emulate Cedric's fucking technique. However, his balance wasn't as good and he ended up planting his knees on each side of Sampson and bouncing his pelvis on the fuck pole.

Hadrian came over and offered his cock to Sampson, who took it with gusto, and then Hadrian got in a push up position, sucking Paulus as he face fucked Sampson with every repetition. The three men had more stamina than any of the other men in the room. They instinctively found a rhythm that was just right for a long fuck.

Maximus, Joshua, and the wresting bears sat together and confessed their desires. Joshua had been attracted to Maximus since Fulvius died and there was no one to care for him. He had felt something special when they fucked by the pool. Joshua had always topped and he wanted to feel his friend's cock in his ass.

Orsinian felt guilty that after a decade of friendship, he had never enjoyed Cedric's cock in his ass. Cedric had let Orsinian shove his cock in the red bear's ass any time and in any position, he wanted. Orsinian never reciprocated. After his experiences with Maximus, he could enjoy it now.

Maximus rolled Joshua on his back, and slowly began to work his cock into the hole. Orsinian got on his hands and knees above Joshua spread his ass for Cedric. Joshua and Orsinian connected cock to mouth, but their asses' were open. Cedric entered Orsinian timidly, but after three or four thrusts realized Orsinian was leaning back on his cock trying to get more in his ass. Maximus watched as Cedric's face glowed with pleasure as his cock went deep in Orsinian's ass.

With Joshua's cock in his mouth Orsinian enjoyed watching Max's thick meat eased its way into Joshua's ass. The hairless hole parted as the red-purple head, dripping with pre-cum, worked in deeper and deeper. Max pulled the entire member out and then eased it in again, allowing Joshua to get accustomed to the foreign object in his ass, and giving his lover a better view of the cock he had enjoyed so much.

Cedric's cock then rammed Orsinian's prostate, and he forgot Maximus. Joshua was relieved it didn't hurt the way he thought it might and relaxed his ass. The slow pumping was comfortable, and he stuck out his tongue to catch the filaments of pre-cum dripping from Orsinian's cock, positioned directly above his head. The taste of the pre-cum and the slow fucking began to have an effect. He pulled his legs back toward his chest to open his ass more. A huge bead of pre-cum emerged from Orsinian's cock and dripped toward Joshua's mouth slowly connected by a thin filament to the piss slit.

Optimus, Otter and Wolf were sitting in the pool enjoying the scene, playing with their cocks. Wolf and Otter fed their cocks to

Optimus. Wolf described the scene as Optimus alternated licking the two cocks.

"Shit, Paulus looks as if he is sitting on a tree trunk," Wolf said. "The thin kid must have some room in his ass, I thought Othacar's horse cock would have gone in his ass and come out his mouth."

Otter added, "I've never seen Julian look so happy. I wouldn't have guessed he could take Badger. Those heavy men have asses of iron. It's hard to wedge a good piece of meat in them."

Arcturus came up and sat next to Optimus, he took a quick lick of Otter's cock, and whispered into Optimus' ear, "I want to fuck. Real bad!"

Optimus said, "Talk to these guys, I don't want to leave them ready to shoot, without anyone to take their load."

"I'll fuck you all!" he replied. Arcturus got up, whispered to Wolf and Otter. After a brief conversation, Optimus tried to pull away from Wolf's cock, but Wolf held his head. Arcturus sat down again. They are ready to play. Optimus got out of the pool and Wolf sat on the floor with his legs wide open and his cock sticking straight up in the air. He told Optimus to suck Wolf's cock and Optimus found himself with his mouth near the floor, sucking Wolf, with his ass in the air. Arcturus spread Optimus' legs wide so the hole was as open and very exposed, shoved two well-oiled fingers into the chute then popped his cock in all the way. Optimus almost came. Arcturus was big, and thick as Maximus and twice as long.

Arcturus wasn't too gentle at all. In his few fuck sessions with Julian, he had figured out what exited him the most and assumed if it was good for him it would be good for Optimus. He pulled all the way out, and then shoved it in all the way in as hard and as deep as he could. After twenty deep thrusts, something gave way in Optimus' ass, his hole opened still wider, and the monster cock went in deeper. He couldn't last much longer. Arcturus pulled out.

Optimus opened his eyes and saw Otter next to him, with his ass in the air, and watched he saw the expression in Otter's eyes as Arcturus filled him up. Optimus realized Otter, the best bottom in the group, was feeling the exact same thing he had felt a moment earlier. Optimus lay down on his back and relaxed.

Arcturus couldn't relax; his engorged cock and sperm filled balls were ready to burst. Arcturus stopped fucking Otter. He quickly lifted Optimus' legs and was deep in his ass again. The thrusts were slower and deeper. Optimus felt sorry for Otter's empty ass, when something warm engulfed his cock. Otter sat on Optimus' cock while Arcturus' cock pumped the magistrate's increasingly sensitive ass. "I'm cumming!" Arcturus shouted as he emptied his fuck tool in the quivering ass. Optimus began squirting in Otter's hole.

Arcturus pulled out, rolled on the floor next to Optimus and kissed him. "That was great!" he said. Then he just stayed still and panted. Otter leaned forward. He was still impaled on Optimus' member and whispered, "I haven't cum yet, and can I shoot in your ass?" Optimus nodded assent. Otter's cock was in Optimus' sperm filled hole immediately. After the monster donkey dong, Optimus' thought Otter's long thin prick would be anticlimactic. The chute was ultra sensitive and tender after the hard fucking. Arcturus had lubricated it with his manly juices. Every movement of Otter's meat was exquisitely pleasurable for both men.

After the stretching exercise, the chute enveloped the smaller cock, molding it to every shape, bend and bulging vein of the cock. Otter's cock was fully erect inside the skin, and Optimus felt his asshole peel back the skin and expose the bulbous cock head. He felt every movement of the cock head into the chute; it poked the prostate several times, and then pulled part of the way out. Optimus opened his eyes and saw Otter was enjoying it as much as he was. Otter began to twitch as he added his load to Arcturus' in Optimus' ass. Otter fell forward cuddling Optimus, and leaving his cock in the ass.

"You know, I could still fuck a horse," Arcturus said. Optimus and Otter laughed. All realized they felt the same way. The night is not over yet.

CHAPTER ELEVEN

Arthur is born

Otter looked up as his cock withdrew from Optimus' ass and saw Cedric was bouncing on Sampson's cock. Paulus' buried his cock deeply in Julian's ass. Maximus' meat was in Orsinian. He couldn't tell who had cum and who hadn't. Clearly all the men were in good form. Hadrian went from man to man with a wineskin and quenched everyone's thirst.

Hadrian had a good sense of the amount of wine needed to keep a party going, without getting everyone so drunk they could not function. Drunken debauches were a part of German rituals and played a role in Celtic tradition, but Hadrian wanted hard cocks. Drunkenness was fine as an excuse for orgies and sexual liberties, but all of these men were unashamed of their sexual prowess and their choice of partners. Men soon filled the bath, relaxing and cleaning off after the intense interlude. The room was warm, the men had climaxed at least once, but they felt a need to keep the feeling going.

Wolf and Badger began to play a drum and a flute, and dance. It was one of the old tribal dances of the east coast. They had bound their cocks in the leather ties, and as the other men joined the dance, they did the same. Wolf began chanting. It was a war dance, used on the eve of battle. The men formed a ring with interlocked arms and took up the chant. Even the blind man joined in, he knew of these dances and once he got the rhythm, never missed a step.

The men danced and chanted under the gold dome of the bath, below the images of dancing gods, and all became aware they wanted to become fucking gods, emulating the upper tier of the frescoes. As they danced, their cocks got harder and harder and they realized release was in their companion's ass.

Hadrian broke out of the group and oiled everyone's cock and hole. Some, like Otter and Optimus hardly noticed. Fox was excited as a finger entered his ass. Othacar-Sampson felt a twinge of fear, but his raging hard on made that seem unimportant. Hadrian rejoined the dancing ring.

Wolf slowed the beating of the drum and stopped, bent over and opened his hole for Hadrian. Hadrian entered and spread his ass for Badger. Fox, Julian, Optimus, Cedric, Maximus, Joshua, Paulus, Orsinian, Arcturus and finally Sampson followed forming a fornicating ring. Sampson grabbed Arcturus' tits as he shoved to the hilt; Wolf deep dicked Sampson's tender ass.

Wolf hit the bull's eye, and Sampson tried to pump deeper into Arcturus' ass and he tried to wiggle his ass to get Wolf's cock deeper into his prostate. He gave out a low growl. The growl became a moan for some of the men, a roar for Arcturus. Badger came first, howling as he filled Hadrian' ass, Optimus next shooting his load into Julian. Wolf, Sampson and Arcturus came together, Wolf holding Sampson in place as he had a convulsive orgasm. Soon every cock was subsiding; everyone had filled a friend's ass with his seed. The night was over, all slept well.

As the small expedition left the next morning, Orsinian pulled Sampson aside and handed him a gift. It was a crescent of gold, smooth at one end and with a dragonhead at the other. "Julian and I made it for you, to fill in the hole." Orsinian said. He handed it to Sampson to feel. I was smooth and well oiled.

"Can you put it in?" Sampson asked. Orsinian opened Sampson's loincloth, took his penis and peeled back the skin. He slowly worked the blunt end into the piss slit, and then through the tunnel until it came out the ring hole. Soon only, the dragonhead peaked out of his slit.

"Sampson Dragon-Cock," Orsinian said. This struck a responsive chord in the blind man's heart. The new ring had been stimulating and now he realized it might be decorative too. Sampson thanked him.

The men set off. Arcturus' in-laws village was two days away, and the men made good time. Badger scouted out the trail. The diminutive man disappeared into the underbrush, covering the areas in advance. Joshua and Paulus followed next and Orsinian and Arcturus made up the rear guard.

"I've never done anything like last night," Arcturus stated. "It was unbelievable. We need more men, but I'd hate to get men who didn't share our interests."

"You didn't know you had that interest until we found you," Observed Orsinian. "You seem to like it. I was wrestling for ten years and never found anyone who seem to object too much to shoving their meat in my hole, and remarkable few who had much trouble taking it in their shit chute."

"I guess you are right, I had no idea. I never thought about fucking or sucking men. Life was so miserable, I didn't think much about anything other than getting through the day," Arcturus said. "There was so much emphasis on fucking women at my father's house, it really didn't occur to me."

"I think we have someone to appeal to all tastes. Young, old, smooth, hairy, average dicked and horse hung. If we encounter anyone who is interested in men, we can get him," said Orsinian.

"Maybe I could attract some men." Arcturus said.

"Shit no!" Orsinian laughed. "You're the bounty for joining! We don't want to waste your cock on men who might not join. I can take care of the potential men. If they have any interest in man sex, they know about wrestlers. I can cull out the unworthy."

The trip was uneventful, as they progressed further west the population increased. Here and there, one found a settlement or villa still functioning as in the old days. More often, you found a villa hastily fortified and surrounded by hovels built by refugees.

Two days later, they reached the territories of Arcturus' in-laws. The small party of men caused a stir wherever they went, but there was excitement at the Villa Augusta, the family home. Arcturus' father in law, Britannicus Learian was a wealthy and powerful man. The villa was professionally fortified and the refugee settlement was orderly and firmly under control. The gatekeeper recognized Arcturus and greeted him warmly, but asked them to stay outside until the family could greet him properly.

The servants brought food and drink. Britannicus appeared with a man Arcturus did not know. "Greeting Arcturus. You are alive!" Britannicus called.

"Yes and you look well It is good to see you safe and in charge!" Arcturus said and then introduced his companions. Britannicus was cordial and introduced his companion as Gildas, a man from the north.

"We thought you were dead. We were told they found your body." Britannicus said, obviously uneasy. "Gwenwyr, your wife was distraught, with your three sons to care for. This world is not good for a woman alone." Clearly, Britannicus was trying to say something important. He seemed to be unwilling to come to the point. Everyone was uneasy.

Gildas spoke up. "I married your wife."

"She was a widow, we were sure you were dead!" reiterated Britannicus. "Gildas is a powerful man. He promised to adopt your children as his own and to make them his heirs! He has kept his word I gave my permission. I'm sorry."

Arcturus realized he had only been dead for six months, and such a quick remarriage was unseemly. There must have been other considerations. Power wealth and security were the needs of the times and Gildas must have provided this for Gwenwyr, and for Britannicus. Arcturus also realized Britannicus did not say he was sorry often; he could have had them killed if he wished.

"A father never needs to apologize for looking after the best interests of his daughter and grand children. These are difficult times;

we must find safety where we can. You are a wise man, Britannicus." The tension eased as Arcturus spoke these words. He stepped forward and grasped Gildas' hand. "But I am afraid Gwenwyr has two husbands."

"We will work something out!" Britannicus bellowed, "We must celebrate! He who was lost is found! It is a great day!" Britannicus liked Arcturus, and his wife, Lady Domina, was Arcturus' mother's cousin. They all entered the villa.

The lawyers were gone; the priest had fled, so the business of resolving the legal problems took some doing. "What if I were to stay dead? My father would never give me my inheritance. I am sure he has mourned enough," Arcturus said with a bitter laugh.

"If you were dead your sons would be your heirs," Britannicus said, thinking aloud. He was always calculating potential benefit to his family. This seemed to be the easiest solution for the problem. With the problem resolved, Arcturus explained the reason for the visit.

Britannicus was careful in his choice of words. He neither accepted nor rejected the request. This was all Arcturus wanted at this time. Britannicus rose and offered a toast. He spoke first of the loss of his son in law Arcturus, who had died fighting the Saxons, and then of the arrival of new comrades lead by…, here he stopped. He needed a name. He thought and said, "Led by Arthur, a great warlord from the east.

The newly christened Arthur rose and gave a tribute to Britannicus, and his son-in-law, Gildas, protector of widows and orphans. The night became festive. The men eventually went to the baths to sober up, and let the women clean up after the banquet.

The well-maintained baths were large for a private villa; the water was warm and clean. As the men striped and entered the water Britannicus and his men couldn't help but notice the visitors. Gildas whispered to Britannicus, "I've never seen so many hung men in my life. It's a freak show in a circus!"

"One hell of a circus," Britannicus replied. He got in the water. He sat next to Paulus on a bench in the warm water. He discovered Paulus' ancestor and was interested in the boy's travels since his father's death. Britannicus had only daughters, and he felt sympathy for the fatherless boy. Britannicus was an older man. He was still big and muscular, with gray hair. He looked like an older version of Othacar, a bit hairier, and more grizzled.

Gildas sat next to Orsinian and soon discovered the wrestler's past. Orsinian asked if he wrestled. "Not any more, I am an old married man now, I don't play in games" Gildas said. He realized this might sound as if he were insulting Orsinian, and he quickly added, "My companions over there still wrestle. I've watched many exciting matches." He waved at two big blond men on the other side of the pool. "Lucas, Leo, come over here!" The two men lumbered over.

After a brief conversation, the two men recognized the name of Orsinian the Armenian Bear, and the conversation became animated. A young muscular man was talking with Joshua and a heavyset older man was all but drooling over Badger. A young man spoke with Arthur.

Arthur could feel the sexual excitement build in the room. He guessed nothing would happen tonight, but if any of the men could find a place to be alone, they would soon have company. He had never seen Britannicus interested in a man before. Paulus looked younger than his age. Perhaps that was the attraction.

The young man talking to Arthur was Decius, a refugee from the east. He and Festus, his father's master of the horse, the man speaking with Badger, had been sent west with valuables to their country home in Wales. When they reached it, other refugees occupied the house. They who did not intend to let the original owners return without a fight. Decius and Festus tried to return home. They were at Britannicus' villa when they learned the eastern part of the country was lost to the Saxons, and so there they stayed.

Decius was well built. There was no trace of boyishness about him. Without a family, he was living on the goodwill and hospitality of Britannicus, He clearly wanted to do battle with the Saxon's and either find his family or avenge them. Arthur knew he would have no trouble recruiting Decius and Festus and getting them away from Britannicus. Hospitality demanded he treat them well, but Britannicus naturally preferred to have only members of his clan in his villa.

Arthur looked at Badger and Festus talking, and noted the look of admiration, or lust in Festus' eyes. Arthur had always thought horsemen liked men who were hung like horses, and horse hung described Badger. Both Arthur and Paulus sported impressive equipment, but Festus couldn't dream of sex with men of their rank. Festus and Badger were of the same class. Decius could look at Arthur as a man of similar station, and Arthur noticed every time he looked away, Decius looked at Arthur's impressive equipment.

The party broke up and the visitors went to a room to sleep in one of the out buildings of the villa. The men discussed the situation. "I bet Lucas and Leo will join our party," Orsinian said. "They are young and strong, Leo is married to a bitch, and I doubt either men care much for women. They will only be servants and farm hands here."

"Do you think they will like our group?" Arthur asked.

"I think so, they are wrestlers, and they were checking me out to decide it they wanted to win or lose!" Orsinian joked.

"And their decision?" Joshua asked.

"I think they could lose to me easily. If Arthur was in the ring, however, I think they would fight like hell to make sure they wouldn't be impaled on your fuck tool!" Orsinian answered. Everyone laughed. "And you Joshua?"

"The man I talked to was Quinton, the youngest son of Gildas' uncle. He has no prospects since everything goes to his brother. He wants loot and honor and maybe cock," Joshua replied.

"The classic dissatisfied younger son," Arthur said. "They are only trouble inside the home, but very useful out. He looks like a strong man."

"Gymnasium strong," Joshua said. "He works at it because he has nothing else to do. I knew scores of men like him at the baths. He may shave himself to look more statue-like. When I told him my name is Joshua, he said I looked more like Hercules."

"Would he be of any use in a battle?" Badger asked.

"Gymnasium strong can convert to battlefield strong. He is ambitious and wants to distinguish himself. He'll be fine," Joshua said.

"Well Festus is a useful man," Badger said. "Knows horses from top to bottom, spent years in the cavalry and knows all about cavalry tactics. He's old, but strong as an ox. I will bet he's a good hunter too." Arthur then told of his conversation with Decius.

"Do you want to hear about Britannicus?" asked Paulus. "I think he may be interested."

"You're kidding!" Arthur said.

"Not at all. Lady Domina is well named indeed. She controls the house with her three daughters. Britannicus is no longer needed since he has reproduced. Gildas is the nail in his coffin. He is the heir. With Gwenwyr and Domina, they will do what they wish. Britannicus knows his time is over, he would love a chance to get away and be free of the women," Paulus explained.

"Pussy whipped," Badger said.

"You must have gotten more out of Britannicus in your brief time in the bath than I did in five years of marriage," Arthur complained.

"I think he likes me," Paulus said. "He was a bit drunk, and he likes me, he told me too much. The bath is the only place he can get away from her. I think he handpicked the guys in the bath, and I bet he has some others lined up to join us." The men went to sleep. It had been a busy day.

The men went on a hunting expedition the next day. Arthur and Orsinian found themselves alone. "Do you think Paulus is right?" asked Arthur.

"I don't know, but I do know Britannicus was mighty taken with Paulus. Paulus is a smart boy. He is young, but he has survived for two years in Saxon territory. I can't believe he misunderstood. He didn't misunderstand Britannicus was playing with his cock under the water," Orsinian answered.

"Are you sure?"

"I was closer than you were. And there was some mutual enjoyment too," Orsinian added. "Paulus was smart enough to look a bit shocked and a bit more excited. He understood exactly what Britannicus wanted."

"Domina's and Britannicus' relationship has never been close, but I thought it was normal marital irritations," Arthur mused. "Gildas is wealthy and powerful, he is the perfect match for future security if you combine their property and my son's, they will have what was a kingdom before the Romans came." He paused. "I will be interested in seeing who shows up a dinner tonight"

"I will be interested in seeing who ends up naked in the baths after dinner," Orsinian added.

The next day Gildas had returned to his home with Gwenwyr, but Lucas and Leo remained behind, with two of their friends, big beefy farmers. Decius and Festus remained. Festus brought two horse trainers with him, Orion and Ursus. Quinton brought two friends with him, Patricius and Bardo. Britannicus was joined by his half brother Lucian, and two cousins, Primus and Alban.

Celtic traditions replaced Roman dignity; the dinner was informal. All of the men mixed without respect to rank. The women left the tables early, leaving the men to themselves.

Men left to themselves meant more wine and beer, and the collection of strangers began to relax and feel comfortable. They adjourned to the baths, and Britannicus stationed servants at the doors to insure privacy.

As soon as the men stripped, Arthur noticed the cock size of the men in the room was greater than it had been the day before. None of the men the day before had small cocks, but today the new members of the group were distinctly well endowed. The horse trainers were big, crude, hairy men with big balls and low swinging cocks. They clearly weren't used to bathing, but didn't mind being naked at all. Big cocks made up for a lot of crudeness.

Quinton's friends were as smooth and gymnasium muscular as he was. Patricius was greyhound. Bardo was a short Hercules with compact balls and cock. Primus and Alban were country bumpkins, big, cheerful men, with never cut hair. Primus had red hair, Alban's was black. They braided their hair. Their beards merged with the thick pelts of hair that covered their bodies. They were probably thin and well built, but only the ends of their cocks hung below the thick bush of their pubic hair.

Lucian came up to Arthur and spoke. "I see that all of my brother's glowing descriptions of you are true. You are a handsome man whose spirit is as attractive as his appearance." His stilted speech was slowly delivered. Arthur realized this was an effort to overcome a speech impediment.

"I appreciate your kind words," Arthur replied. "You are obviously a man of culture and civilization; I have enjoyed meeting you tonight. The times must be difficult for a man of your education and breeding."

"I was a merchant on the coast, and lost everything I owned when the Saxons invaded. My wife died in the flight from Dover, we had no children, which is perhaps a blessing in these evil times. I am alone." Lucian said.

"I am so sorry. But Britannicus is your brother?" Arthur asked.

"Half brother, but we were raised apart. He is a kind and generous man. He had no need to help me in my hour of need," Lucian added. "I have helped him wherever I could in the protection of this place. I admit sword and spear and bow and arrows were as foreign to my old life as they are a part of me now. I am a much stronger man now than when I fled the coast."

Lucian carefully enunciated every word. He clearly was offering his services. Arthur suspected years of ridicule for his speech impediment left him fearful of being embarrassed. He was trying to avoid the problem. He was an impressive big man, and the contrast between his lisp and size was almost comic. "Britannicus has explained to you our needs?" Arthur asked.

"Oh yeth!" he said. "I know and I want to join you."

"Have you ever fought?" Arthur asked.

"Never, but I have nothing to lose in death. I would rather die killing Saxons than hiding in Wales!" Lucian said.

"I can agree with you there!" Arthur said. "Are your cousins as eager as you to fight the Germans?"

Lucian laughed. "There are few barbarians more barbaric than those boys. They make the blue men of the north look like Egyptian eunuchs," he added. "Actually, I refused to believe they were related to me when I first met them. Some aunt's daughter married someone in an out of the way part of the island and there they are." He laughed, and whispered into Arthur's ear. "There are actually two intelligent and strong men under all that hair. No education at all, but good boys."

"Do they have a cock, or balls hidden in all that hair?" Arthur asked. He wanted to see how Lucian reacted.

Without batting an eye or hesitating, Lucian replied. "They sport four good sized balls and two more than good sized cocks." Arthur and Lucian looked each other in the eye, and understood. "They are good men to have with you in a camp. They're very friendly." He called the boys over.

They were all in the pool up to their necks in water. Lucian directed Arthur's hands into Primus and Alban's crotches and told him to dig in. He whispered to the two hairballs that Arthur hadn't been sure they were fully equipped. Both laughed heartily and seemed to enjoy groping.

"We're real men!" Alban said under his breath, "And you look like a real man too." Alban gripped Arthur's balls, and Primus took hold of his cock. Arthur located both of the men's cocks by then and felt them as they began to engorge. Lucian was behind them and Arthur was sure their cousin was working a finger or two into the men's asses.

On the other side of the pool, Britannicus sat with Paulus, Quinton, Bardo and Patricius. They sat on an underwater bench that left only their shoulders above the warm water. In the dim flickering light of the bath, the men could barely see each other. Britannicus had one arm around Paulus and held him close. Joshua joined the group and stood behind Bardo.

Between the two groups of men, Badger and the horsemen were frolicking. They were making quite a bit of noise and they made it difficult to hear in the room for more than a few feet. Badger quickly found out all of the men liked close physical contact, but they could continue to play, even in a state of sexual arousal.

Orsinian sat with Lucas, Leo, and their friends known only by their nicknames Rooster and Goatman. They all liked to wrestle, and seem to have been village champions as far as Orsinian could tell. They spoke the dialect of the area and were hard to understand.

Britannicus rose and called an end to the night. The men reluctantly got out of the water and dried off. When the men returned to their quarters, they again discussed the night's events.

"The water may have been placid, but beneath the surface there was a lot of activity," Arthur said.

"I wonder if there is a spy hole somewhere, Britannicus seemed both very interested and very cautious," Orsinian observed. "If those men weren't prospective recruits, I misunderstood the situation completely."

"He told me he has something planned for tomorrow," Paulus said. "It is a hunt of some sort. My guess is he wants to get away from the women so we can talk."

"Unless I misunderstood something," Badger said, "it's more than talk he is after."

CHAPTER TWELVE

New Friends

The next morning Britannicus announced a hunt. The plan was for the men to break into groups, separate hunting parties and then return a day later. Britannicus took the two younger men, Decius and Paulus with him. Arthur, Lucian, Primus and Alban made up the second group. Orsinian lead the group of wrestlers; Joshua, the muscle men, Quinton, Patricus and Bardo, and Badger the horsemen, Festus, Orion and Ursus. Arthur noticed the men matched well and shared common interests.

The men broke up and went in different directions. It was an exceptionally warm and sunny day for early winter. It was actually comfortable in the sun, and there was no need for the heavy cloaks and robes of the season.

As they moved farther and farther away from the villa and Lady Domina, Britannicus became more British and less Roman. He was less formal and almost boy like in his enjoyment of the hunt. He knew the area well and found a secluded spot overlooking a deer path through the woods. He stationed Decius on one side of the path, and took Paulus to the other. The men lay down for the long wait for a deer to pass by.

Britannicus had groped Paulus in the bath. While Paulus had seemed shocked, his huge member began to swell immediately, and he took no measures to remove his hand. The boy had also seemed excited at joining the older man in the hunt. Britannicus stripped down to a loincloth and his hunting bow in the warmth of the day. Paulus did the same, and the two men lay down next to each other on Britannicus' bear cloak he spread on the ground.

"How long does it usually take before you spot a deer?" Paulus asked.

"If we are lucky only half a day," whispered Britannicus. He put his arm around Paulus, who was thin and looked cold. "Hunting is the most boring sport in the world until it turns into the most exciting one."

"Do you hunt often? Running the villa must be a full time operation," Paulus asked as he snuggled closer to the big man.

"I try too, but it is difficult. The women run the house, but they don't like me out of the place. I think they are afraid I might enjoy myself," Britannicus said with a touch of bitterness. "They seem to think I am too old." Paulus shivered a bit, and Britannicus rose up and let Paulus slip half under him. Paulus enjoyed the heat of the big man. Britannicus straddled Paulus leg, with his cock pressed against the ass cheek. He slowly humped Paulus leg.

Paulus felt comfortable with the big man. While he looked nothing like his father, his power and authority brought back old memories. Paulus had felt stranded and Britannicus' local connections and family were major assets in the uncertain world. They needed men like him if they were to succeed in repelling the Saxons. Paulus felt the older man's cock get harder and harder, and realized he wanted Britannicus as much as Britannicus wanted him.

Britannicus adjusted his position and let Paulus get up. Paulus stretched and sat down cross-legged before Britannicus, who was on his stomach. Britannicus wiggled closer, took off the boy's loincloth and began sucking the huge cock. He only stopped when Paulus climaxed and filled his mouth with milky fluid. He had never sucked a man before, and never taken a load.

"I'm sorry." Paulus said. "I didn't know I was that close."

"I've never enjoyed anything so much in my life!" Britannicus said. "Did I do it right?"

"If you are drinking cum, you did something right," Paulus said as he smiled.

Leading the second group Lucian was a good guide. Arthur noted that for a city man he had learned the ways of the countryside well. The day was remarkably warm, and the men stripped to loincloths. Primus and Alban were one with the forest. They were scouting in advance and disappeared. Even half-naked, the hairy men merged with the dark woods.

"I am surprised you get along so well with your cousins. They seem so crude," Arthur said to Lucian.

"Our first meeting was difficult," Lucian said. "Britannicus sent me out with them to learn how to hunt. Alban went ahead, and Primus was making fun of my lisp. He though the lisp and my urban ways meant I was effeminate. He got ruder and ruder and more vulgar, and then he jumped me." Lucian continued. "Much to his surprise, I was a lot stronger than he thought, and instead of him raping me, I sank my cock into his ass."

"He ran away, and came back with Alban. I wasn't sure I could beat the two of them, but I was too proud to run. I stood my ground. We stared at each other and then Alban asked if I could do to him what I had just done to Primus," Lucian smiled.

Arthur laughed, "You must have hit a good spot."

"I must have!" Lucian said. "I had introduced Primus to a whole group of sensations and feelings he didn't know he had. Alban liked it too. They tried fucking each other later, but it was my cock that seemed to turn their asses into a magic tunnel."

"Magic tunnel? That's a new word for it!" Arthur laughed again.

"Magic tunnel is the phrase their tribe uses to describe the road to heaven," Lucian explained. "I sometimes suspect they think I am a high priest fucking them into the next world! I could see their minds working when they felt your cock in the pool. They may be ready to anoint you the Pontfex Maximus! Incidentally, they have been very pleasant ever since I introduced them to the joys of anal sex. They need big cocks to make them happy. I am the biggest man at the Villa. Until your arrival, of course."

"You noticed?" Arthur asked.

"I thought we both noticed each other's... assets?" Lucian said.

Arthur smiled and said, "I thought I was staring at your cock."

"Frankly," Lucian said, "I was staring and trying not to drool. I was trying not to embarrass myself." Arthur turned and felt Lucian's cock through the loincloth. Lucian dropped to his knees. He removed Arthur's loincloth, and began kissing the enlarging cock. Lucian got his tongue inside the skin licked the cock head. As his cock began to swell, Arthur realized Lucian was doing what Wolf enjoyed so much. Lucian's tongue was licking the underside of his cock, while sharing the inside of the skin with Arthur's monster cock head.

"That's good!" Arthur said. "Do I need to save my sperm for your cousins later tonight?"

"I hate to say it, but that is probably a good idea," Lucian said. "Your cock is wonderful. All of you are wonderful!" Lucian stood. Arthur realized the man was very excited, and we could trust Lucian. It took great will power for him to pull his tongue out of Arthur's cock.

"What are Britannicus' intentions?" Arthur asked.

"Actually, he planned this hunting trip for me to ask you what your intentions are should Britannicus join your party," Lucian said. "He doesn't expect to be the leader, but needs to be assured of being of an appropriate rank."

"That shouldn't be a problem," Arthur said, "Tell me more about what is going on."

"The situation at the villa is deteriorating for Britannicus. Lady Domina is getting stronger and stronger. The tribe was once matriarchal, and might be reverting to old traditions. Domina and your former wife are not evil women. They won't poison him in the

Roman manner, but slow suffocation is more their mode. He has less and less power as each day advances." As Lucian told his story, Arthur dropped to his knees and began sucking the older man's impressive member.

Lucian continued. "Britannicus has been looking for a way out, with honor and dignity. Your visit provides the opportunity. He has assembled the men he trusts, or who do not fit in Lady Domina's scheme, and hopes to bring them to you." Fully erect now Lucian oozed pre-cum at a good rate. "I'm afraid I may shoot soon"

"Is that a problem?" Arthur asked.

"Not for me," Lucian said. "I helped Britannicus select likely men. I selected men who were reliable and not too dominated by women. I suspect most are much more interested in men." He began twitching, and flooded Arthur's mouth with man juice. He had to swallow twice to keep from choking. Arthur kept sucking until the twitching subsided, then stood. Lucian kissed him, and was surprised to taste his own cum in Arthur's mouth.

"When did you shoot last? That was more cum in one load than I have ever had," Arthur said. "Is there anything left in your balls?"

"I'm sorry. I didn't want to choke you," Lucian said. "They fill up fast, no one had drunk the juice before, and I usually shoot it in the ass."

"You don't need to apologize. I need to introduce you to Fox back at the villa," Arthur said. "You can tell Britannicus he will be my Master of the soldiers, the second in command," Primus and Alban appeared.

"We have found a deer trail," Primus said. The group followed him into the forest.

With the third group, Joshua realized the men he was with weren't accustomed to the forest. Their hunting experience must have been limited to grand and social hunts, where servants prepared the game in advance for easy capture. Joshua maintained a fast pace from just after dawn until midday, when they stopped to rest.

He wanted to see if the muscle men had any stamina, recalling the men in the gymnasium who could perform great feats of strength once, but only once. Bardo and Patricus seemed fine. Quinton seemed winded. All sat down to eat the bread they brought with them, except Bardo who continued to search the area.

"I haven't seen a trace of anything we could hunt or eat," Quinton complained. "It may be nuts and roots for us tonight."

"I'm afraid we may have been moving too fast," Joshua suggested. "The noise may have spooked the game."

Bardo returned. "Boars!" he whispered. The men grabbed their javelins and bows. Joshua carried a military type spear. Bardo explained the situation and described the location of the animals. "If two of you can go to the west, there is a clear trail to the east. If you scare them, they should follow the trail and we can get them." Joshua and Quinton went to the west. Patricus and Bardo flanked the trail on the east.

Joshua noted Quinton was no longer tired, and was much better about moving silently through the forest. After a short while, they spotted the boars, a huge male and at least three sows. They waited until they felt Bardo and Patricus had time to be in place. They then noisily advanced toward the animals.

They heard a squeal in the distance and assumed a javelin had met its mark. They raced to meet up with the other half of the party. They found Patricius standing over the body of a sow. It was a big animal, and Joshua realized it was a great catch. "Bardo's chasing the rest of the boars," he said. They all raced after him.

They arrived on a scene that recalled the many depictions of Hercules and the Boar. The boar had stopped and turned to charge the hunter. Bardo and the boar were facing each other. Bardo lowered his spear. The boar charged. Bardo dropped to his knee planting the spear in the ground. The boar essentially skewered himself on the spear. Bardo jumped away, since the force of the changing animal could have hurt him even when the animal was wounded. Quinton rushed forward and slit the thrashing animal's throat.

They embraced in joy. It was a triumph. Many men went a lifetime without getting a boar and in a few moments, these inexperienced men had two. "How are we going to get these monsters back to the villa?" Joshua asked.

"Britannicus will send servants to fetch them." Patricius said. "We need to gut them and hang them up so nothing else will eat them before the servants arrive." None of the men knew how to gut a boar, so they dragged the male boar to the area next to the sow, sat and rested.

They heard noises and hid, but soon recognized Orsinian's booming voice. It turned out Orsinian's group was also following the boars' trail. Lucas and Leo knew exactly what to do with the two dead animals, strung them up, and gutted them with a minimum of mess. Goatman and Rooster clearly knew what parts of the boars were useful and went to a nearby stream to wash the inner organs and store them in the cold water. Bardo and Quinton helped the farmers clean the animals covering themselves in blood and gore. They went to the stream to clean up in the cold water.

As the sun set the warmth of the day disappeared. Orsinian started a fire and cooked three pheasants they caught earlier in the day. Each man had bread and wine from the villa, and Joshua had brought extra brought wine and nuts. The men who bathed were freezing cold, Orsinian invited them to share his robe and furs, and they formed a tent with these and some branches. It was open to the heat of the fire on one side. They were naked with their clothes drying near the fire. Joshua did the same with the body builders and they formed a tight cluster around the fire.

Everyone was in a good mood. Lucas caught some fish in the stream, and brought some apples. For most of the men, the simple dinner was a feast beyond imagining. Ordinary people rarely ate meat. They also were surprised by Orsinian and Joshua's treatment of them. To Lucas and Leo, these were men of rank, comrades of a powerful chieftain. They were accustomed to being treated as plebs, little more than dirt.

Here there was respect and perhaps brotherly comradeship. The men talked well into the night discussing the hunt, and the Saxon peril. Inside the little tents, body heat maintained the warmth. They collected the dried clothes and used them as blankets. As the fire died down, Orsinian and Joshua used their clothes to seal the door. Bodybuilders were in one tent, wrestlers in the other.

Orsinian had just closed his eyes when he felt someone take his cock in his mouth. The man was an expert cocksucker, and Orsinian thanked him.

"Oh shit, you aren't Goatman?" Rooster said.

"Orsinian here, but don't stop." Orsinian replied.

"With all this bathing, I can't even identify my friend anymore." Rooster complained.

A voice on the other side of Orsinian asked. "Who in hell am I sucking then?" It was Goatman.

"Leo," another voice answered. Everyone laughed.

"Lucas, are you the only one here getting any sleep?" Orsinian asked.

"Yes," he answered. It was pitch dark in the tent, so Orsinian didn't know whom he sucked during the night. Rooster got his first load. He was quite sure he fucked either Leo or Lucas, and guessed Goatman was the man who fucked him. It was a good night.

In the next tent, Bardo cuddled next to Joshua. Quinton and Patricius were at Joshua's back. Bardo wiggled his ass to stimulate Joshua's cock. Joshua slowly worked his cock into the boar killer's hole. He felt the little Hercules stiffen up, then relax as Joshua's big cock head worked its way deeper into the chute.

"Can you leave it in there all night?" Bardo asked.

"I can try," Joshua answered. Joshua's cock wasn't that big, but it was long, and the head was huge. Bardo had incredibly tight ass muscles, so once Joshua was in, Bardo clamped down and trapped the cock in the chute. Joshua and Bardo had a good night. Periodically Joshua would pump a few times. Bardo would respond by tightening his hole and squeezing the cock, forcing it deeper into his ass. Each man made it through the night without an orgasm, but in a state of great sexual stimulation.

If Britannicus planned the hunting trip as a way for men to get to know each other, this trip was a spectacular success. All of the hunting parties regrouped in a clearing to the west of the villa. They piled three deers, two boars and many smaller animals and birds in a clearing.

The men were friends now, confident in each other's abilities. Domina and her daughters would never know the reasons for the new comradeship. Arthur's little army had doubled in size. There was another festive banquet to greet the returning hunters, and Arthur announced his departure. Britannicus would follow a month later with his troop. After the dinner, the period in the baths was quiet. They all went to bed early. The night before had been fun, but not restful.

Arthur left early the next morning, loaded up with food for the trip and the best wishes of Britannicus and his friends. Orsinian walked next to Arthur.

"How many of them did you fuck?" he asked with a twinkle in his eye.

"Only Primus and Alban, Lucian says they think of me as a demigod," Arthur said. "Otter could learn a few things from those men. To say they were enthusiastic about being fucked is an understatement."

"I played stud, and they played mare for the whole night!" Badger said. "They are good men. We should send them out to the Saxon ships and have them exhaust the barbarians with their insatiable need to screw. The Saxons would not be strong enough to hold up a sword!"

"It was a long night?" Arthur asked.

"A good night," Badger said. "I bottomed for Festus just to get off my feet."

"A kindness to the elderly?" Orsinian said.

"At first I was being nice, but Festus is good. I think he's had practice. I found myself enjoying it, and then more than enjoying it," Badger said. "I ended up sleeping with him."

"How was Britannicus?" Arthur asked.

"He's a good man, a lot like Fox in some ways." Paulus said.

"It will be good to get home." Arthur said. He realized he now thought of the villa by the sea as his home.

CHAPTER THIRTEEN

Return to the Villa

At midday, the group heard a rustling to their rear and they hid, sending Badger back to see who or what was coming. He quickly returned with Lucian, Primus and Alban.

"Greetings Arthur!" Lucian called. "Britannicus sent us to join you. He felt we could help scout out the area"

"Join us friends!" Arthur said. "It is always good to have companions on a long trip." As Lucian caught up with them, Arthur said under his breath. "I assume you were sent as a spy?"

"As always you are a perceptive man." Lucian said. "However, treachery is not part of my nature, nor Britannicus'. He just likes to be safe."

A day later, the group arrived at the villa. There was considerable joy at the return, and the success of the mission. There had been several changes at the villa. The twins, Theo and Marcus had departed to try to get back to Hispania. A group of their compatriots had passed by the villa. They were planning to get a boat in Cornwall to take them back to their home province. The winter weather was stormy, but the seas were free of Saxons, so they decided to join the group.

Lucian was immediately attracted to Maximus and Optimus. They were all city men, and had the same experiences. Primus and Alban quickly bonded with Wolf and Otter. Within a day, it was as if they were brothers. Curiously, they also seemed to get along with Sampson. Optimus thought it was because they all spoke Latin equally badly. Optimus was not aware of the tribal legends of a blind hero and his companion dragon. Primus and Alban first encountered Sampson emerging from the thermal pool with the golden dragon ornament shimmering in his cock head.

At midwinter, the men had little to do except hunt and fish and watch. Arthur, Maximus and Sampson planned. The Saxon's would normally send a scouting ship out in late winter. These would select a landing place and spy on the natives before returning to bring the main party. Arthur planned to destroy this ship, and leave the main party without reconnaissance.

Without this information, Sampson thought they would return to the same site as the last year. They would then try to lure the main group into an unfavorable site for a battle.

Julian had his forge producing weapons at a brisk pace. The villa was well fortified now. It was invisible from the sea, and difficult to find on the landside. Hadrian, the former butler, was a paragon of domestic economy and efficiency. He knew what foods could be stored and what would go bad. With Optimus' Roman gentleman's knowledge of farming, they planted winter crops to harvest early and stored for a possible siege.

Wolf had captured several more dogs and was training them to be war dogs. This too was an ancient British tradition. The fearsome Wolfhounds could disrupt an enemy attack and seemed to instill fear.

Lucian felt he had returned home at the villa. He found cultured friends who shared his experiences. The luxury of the place dazzled Primus and Alban, but they found the men very much to their liking. They had been uncomfortable in the female dominated household of Britannicus. Wolf, Fox, Otter and Badger were men they understood. Arthur and Sampson were almost god like to them. Julian outfitted them with fantastical weapons and they felt themselves to be companions of heroes.

While Optimus, Maximus and Lucian were recreating the orderly Roman world they had lost, Primus, Alban and many of the other men were living the life of Celtic myth. They saw the villa filled with great heroes, enchanting weapons, vile enemies, and a sense of brotherhood uniting them in a common cause. Perhaps they would have been happier slaying a multi headed dragon, but they were more than willing to kill a slew of Saxons. A common desire to force the Saxons back into the sea united both groups, the Romans and the Celts.

Primus and Alban liked the food. Maximus was a good cook, and dinner seemed like a banquet to the two men. They didn't understand the desire of all of the men to bathe. They followed Wolf and Fox into the thermal pool, and soon discovered they had an interest in it too. Their sexual experiences had been limited, but enjoyable. In the flickering lights under the golden dome of the pool, they broadened their experiences and their enjoyment.

The warmth of the water surprised them as they got in, far warmer than the hypocausts could achieve at Britannicus home. Then Fox dunked his head under the water and sucked Alban's cock while Wolf played with Primus's member. Fox emerged and dunked again, snagging Primus' half-erect cock.

When Fox emerged a second time Alban asked, "What were you doing? It felt good."

"I think the technical term is cock sucking," Wolf said with a smile. "You've never had that done before?"

"No, it was great!" Primus said.

"Where did you boys learn about sex?" Fox asked. "Watching animals?"

"Yes."

"Wolf, it's time for you and me to give these boys some lessons," Fox said. "No one has ever drained your cock? Sucked your juice out through the piss slit?"

Primus and Alban looked puzzled. "Does it hurt?" Primus asked.

"Fox, Christian charity demands we help these boys out." Wolf said as he got out of the water and lifted Alban onto the edge. Fox deep throated the cock immediately. Fox pulled Primus to the edge, returned to the water and began sucking.

Otter came into the room leading Sampson. The light of the lamps struck the dragon head wedged in his cock. "Do I hear the sucking sounds of enjoyment?" Sampson asked.

"Believe it or not, we have some cock virgins here!" Fox said. "Untouched by human mouths."

"Are they ass virgins too? Otter asked. The two new men were too busy enjoying the new experiences to answer. More men entered the room. Primus and Alban found themselves the focus of good natured and ribald attention. Everyone was willing to help with the men's education. Primus and Alban quickly climaxed under the expert skills of Fox and Wolf. They thought the night was over.

They sat in pool talking. Sampson sat between the two men with by Otter and Wolf. Fox had wandered off in search of more cock to suck. Sampson was rubbing their bodies, trying to feel a sense of their appearance.

"Did you like it?" Wolf asked. He knew the answer; the hairy men must have been lighter since they had spewed so much cum. "Would you like to try it yourselves?"

"It felt good, really good," Alban said. "It's hard for me to think of a cock in my mouth." He lowered his voice.

"Maybe you need to taste the dragon first?" Sampson suggested. Alban looked interested. The dragon peaking out of the big man's cock intrigued him. Sampson of course didn't see this, but he did feel a reaction in Alban's cock. Sampson didn't press the issue. They asked how he became blind. He told them the story, and then the story of Sampson. Christianity had not yet touched the part of Britain these men came from, but they found the stories immensely interesting.

They in turn told the story of the bind hero and his companion dragon. Arthur was sitting with Optimus and Lucian behind the men listening. "I wonder if the dragon story could be used to our advantage," Optimus mused. "Had you ever heard the stories before?"

"Yes, nursery stories in the more cultured areas," Arthur said. "They must be more real in the hinterlands. It might indeed be useful to us."

"Sampson, are there similar legends in your lands?" Optimus asked.

"Come to think of it, there are. The father of Siegfried was a blind king," Sampson answered. "He is like your Hercules."

Optimus mused. "Our newly renamed Arthur is an orphan, without a family. A blind king with a dragon in his cock might be the ideal progenitor." Sampson hooted in laughter.

"Yes!" the blind man said. "Born without woman from the mating of a blind king and a dragon."

Arthur joined in the fun. "I can hear the village wise men and poets reciting the story of the miraculous birth of Arthur!" Arthur recalled the odd story the Twins told of Othacar-Sampson's tribal customs. "How many warriors of your tribe carry your seed in their ass?"

"All of the ones I could catch!" Sampson answered, still laughing.

Paulus joined in, "I can tell you a nice long ride on Sampson's cock is a near mystical experience!"

"I can't catch any men anymore, but I still have a lot of seed, and would gladly share it!" Sampson said. "My tribe thought it gave you strength."

"Well, I felt stronger!" Paulus said. "The incredible orgasm I had. It didn't even tire me out! I wouldn't mind trying it again."

"I would be proud to be your son, Sampson." Arthur said. "And I wouldn't mind taking more of your seed." Arthur said this in a serious tone of voice. Sampson understood, and Arthur had the strange sensation of thinking there were tears in Sampson's nonexistent eyes. "But someone needs to take the dragon out of your cock!" Arthur said in his earlier bantering voice "Alban, Primus, can you help me out here?" Lucian was watching, and wished his cousins could have at least a brief glint of understanding in their eyes. Otter explained to them, "You need to get the dragon out of Sampson's cock."

"How?" Alban asked.

"I think the best way is to suck it out," Wolf said, having great difficulty containing his mirth. "Get your mouths on the cock and start sucking!" They obeyed. They weren't skilled cock suckers, and were very tentative in their approach to the blind man's huge cock. Their inept approach was curiously exciting to Sampson and everyone watching. The laughter increased with the level of sexual excitement.

In the midst of all the laughter, Sampson whispered to Arthur, "You're not making a fool of me, are you?"

"Othacar, I would be honored to be your son," Arthur said. "You are the father I wish I had." Sampson looked relieved. "But as for taking your seed, I'm horny as hell, and your cock is the only one that can scratch the itch I have!"

"Scratch it I will!" Sampson said, and under this breath, he said, "Thank you."

Julian and Hadrian were watching the scene with great amusement. It was clear Primus and Alban were trying to avoid sucking the cock head, but there was no possibility to extract the gold dragon except through the piss slit.

"Those boys need more passion in their lives," Julian observed. Alban bent over trying to suck Sampson's cock. Julian walked over and shoved his cock into the open asshole. It was as if wasp bit a placid horse and suddenly bolted. Alban attacked the cock with enthusiasm. Hadrian saw the reaction and immediately fucked Primus, with the same result.

Alban emerged with the dragon between his teeth. There was general applause. Primus was not willing to give up his crazed worship of the cock. A few moments before he had been unwilling to touch it, now he regretted not being able to deep throat the whole thing.

Hadrian and Julian redirected the two men to other cocks. The main attention in the room focused on Sampson and Arthur. Paulus arrived with some oils and coated Sampson with it, and Sampson took some and worked it into Arthur's ass. Arthur wondered if Hadrian had been giving him lessons. Sampson had the same delicate way of probing an ass that Hadrian did.

Arthur straddled the cock and dropped on it in one smooth movement. There again was applause, and some cheers. By then all of the men were engaged in their own sexual activities, and Arthur and Sampson were soon in their own world.

Arthur had felt some affection for the German Chieftain, and a lot of pity for the man's sorry state, but when Sampson's cock slid into his ass, he felt only lust. When the German donkey dong rammed Arthur's magic nut it felt as if a dam had broken. His entire body was flooded with intense feelings of affection, pleasure and something Arthur would later think was pure, total sexual involvement.

He felt his body melt around the huge cock. His ass relaxed to let it penetrate still deeper. He suddenly felt afraid to move. He was afraid the feelings would go away and vanish.

"Is it good?" Sampson asked. Arthur couldn't talk. He leaned forward and kissed Sampson. They embraced, and eventually Sampson rolled Arthur over and began fucking him with abandon. Arthur could hardly breathe as Sampson wildly fucked him until he roared and shot off, filling Arthur's ass with his warm cream. Arthur shot off too, and the men collapsed on the marble floor. Sampson felt Arthur subside, caressed him and discovered the pools of cum on his chest. Sampson licked up every drop of Arthur's cum before the two men fell asleep.

That night Arthur became the son of a king who mated with a dragon. Primus and Alban discovered the joys of cock sucking. Optimus and Lucian became close friends. Optimus and Maximus had been lovers for years. Maximus' slow and easy approach to fucking had broadened his friendships. He would never have believed it possible, but now an incredibly tight sexual bond linked him and Orsinian. Orsinian's ass loved Maximus' cock. Maximus' cock felt the same way about Orsinian. The cock led the way, but the rest of the body, and eventually the affections followed.

Optimus understood this, and was a generous man. Lucian and Optimus were both well hung bottoms. Later, they decided bottoms who could top were the best fuckers. They understood the feeling of the men they screwed, and could enjoy not only the sensation emanating from their cocks, but also vicariously enjoy the pleasure of the man they fucked.

They watched Arthur and Sampson couple and casually fondled each other, getting hotter and hotter. Optimus felt Lucian's excitement grow as his finger got nearer the asshole. Lucian opened wide and Optimus worked his cock in. Optimus pushed slowly, and Lucian loved the slow progress of the organ in his ass.

Lucian was unaccustomed to the open sex at the villa. He had the Greek feeling a man wasn't naked until his cock head was exposed. He had been shocked at Sampson's public display of his cock head with the embedded dragon. Optimus was fully erect, with his head still covered with the skin. Lucian's tight hole peeled back the skin as Optimus entered. This seemed seemly to Lucian, as the most sensitive part of Optimus' anatomy slowly moved deeper into the chute, the entire passage came alive with new sensations. The cock was big and a bit uncomfortable, but so stimulating, he couldn't imagine anything more exciting.

Optimus fucked for a while then stopped. "Let's trade places?" he asked. They did, and Lucian tried to emulate the other man's technique. It was a new world of sensation for Lucian. It was a different experience from the energetic screwing of Primus and Alban. He had to admit inside the sphincter the sophisticated Optimus was no more soft and welcoming than the crude and oafish Primus and Alban. His cock felt at home lodged in Optimus' ass. He was musing and thinking as he slowly pumped. He had never taken his time before and he started to ejaculate. The first contraction surprised him. There was a pause, then the second ejaculation, another pause, than a third.

They built up strength as they progressed, and by the sixth shot, he still felt there was a supply of man juice trapped in his balls. The seventh contraction let loose a flow and milky seed into Optimus' ass. Optimus was shooting too. Lucian didn't care that Optimus' bloated cock head was free of the enveloping skin for everyone to see. They slept together that night.

The annual German invasion fleet would set sail in early spring. The residents of the villa had months to rest and prepare for the onslaught. Britannicus would join them for the spring battle. Until then sleep and sex were the best way to spend the winter hours.

ABOUT THE AUTHOR

Bob Archman lives in rural Virginia in the shadow of the Blue Ridge and finds writing gay themed adventure fantasies a pleasant way to spend time. He is interested in older, mature men many of whom aren't conventionally regarded as attractive. He discovered many years ago not even gay men can stay young forever. Bob is interested in stories about everyday working men who don't fit the stereotyped images of gay men.

Bob Archman is also the Author of *Clydedale & Company, Clydesdale Goes to the Hunt, Clydesdale Goes to a Funeral* and *The Cave of the Blue Bear*. Available from Amazon.com, TheNazcaPlainsCorp.com or your local bookstore.

Archman

CLYDESDALE & COMPANY

Clydesdale
& COMPANY

A NOVEL BY
Bob Archman

A
BONER
BOOK

Clydesdale
GOES TO THE HUNT

A NOVEL BY
Bob Archman

Archman

CLYDESDALE GOES TO THE HUNT

A BONER BOOK

Archman

Clydesdale
GOES TO A FUNERAL

CLYDESDALE GOES TO A FUNERAL

A NOVEL BY
Bob Archman

A
BONER
BOOK

Archman

The Cave of the Blue Bear

The Cave of the
Blue Bear

a novel by
Bob Archman

www.ingramcontent.com/pod-product-compliance
Lightning Source LLC
Chambersburg PA
CBHW051141260626
47170CB00005B/1917